A Box

Bing bong. The doorbell.

I listen, but nothing happens.

Bing bong. The doorbell again.

My baby brother, Syd, pauses. He's feeding dinosaurs to the laundry bin. He smiles and hands me a slimy stegosaurus.

Bing bong, bing bong, bing bong.

Rats. Mum must be deaf or something.

I lower myself from the top bunk, headfirst. I've got the sheet wrapped round my waist. It's how I'd like to escape from a burning house, but this time all the bedding comes with me and I end up

1

crashing to the floor.

Bing bong!

"Coming!" I yell. I pull on some jeans and peer out of the window. I can only just see through the glass because all the rain there ever was seems to be trying to fall on our house, and most of it's racing down my window. There's a battered half-timbered car wedged between the large concrete rectangles that make up the watercress beds at the back of our house. Mr Hammond, the watercress-bed man, is talking to whoever it is, pointing at our front door, but I can't actually see anybody.

I don't recognise the car and, for one second, I wonder if something exciting might be about to happen. Perhaps someone's come to tell me I've won something.

I drag on yesterday's dirty T-shirt, and try to remember if I ever did enter the Sugar Puffs "Honey Monster challenge" or whether the cardboard packet's still stuck behind the toaster. I'm pretty sure it's stuck behind the toaster.

Putting my hands on the banisters, and without using my feet, I slide over Syd's stair gate and arrive silently at the bottom of the stairs.

I look round for Mum. She's doing her morning

yoga with earplugs. She hasn't even heard the door.

I stop in the hallway, looking out.

Somebody's standing on the other side of the glass, pressing against it; but because our front door's made of this ancient cloudy glass with little ships on, I can only see a shadow. I'm guessing they don't have an umbrella and they're trying to get out of the rain.

Bing bong.

For a moment I wonder if it's a mad axe murderer, but then decide that mad axe murderers probably never call at nine o'clock on a Saturday morning.

I look again at the shadow. I don't think it's a scary shadow, it's really no taller than I am.

I'll take a chance.

I yank open the front door.

"Scarlett? Scarlett McNally?" It's a round shiny man in a sheepskin jacket, with a Father Christmas beard. He is definitely not a mad axe murderer but he doesn't look like he's come to tell me I've won anything. He looks more like someone buying watercress. I'm sure people who tell you you've won something drive cars that were built this century. He's holding a box.

"Yes?" I say, looking round at Mum, who's

stretching now. She still hasn't noticed anything but I expect I can handle this.

"Morning, Scarlett. I was your father's solicitor." He's standing right in the doorway now; half of his jacket's dark with the rain.

Solicitor?

I don't know what to say, so I stare at the man. I go on staring at him. I can stare at people for ages, and they can never do it back anything like as well. It gives me the upper hand. I can see he's getting uncomfortable, so I give him a chance and blink.

He's looking really confused now. "I'm acting on your father's instructions."

"Dad's — but he's..."

"Yes, Scarlett, but he left these items in my care, to be given to you on, or around, your eleventh birthday. You were eleven last week, weren't you?" He grips the box as if he's about to whisk it away.

"Yes — Tuesday."

"Well, happy birthday last Tuesday. It's yours now." He plonks the box on the carpet, fumbles for the door handle, touches his hat and trips out through the door.

"Why did I have to be eleven?" I ask, calling into the rain.

"Haven't a clue – perhaps he thought you'd be old enough to avoid some of his less lovely friends?" He scuttles back to his car, his shoulders hunched against the rain. "Don't get too excited." The door squeaks as he clambers in and when he closes it, a small piece of wood pings off the side.

Reversing, he narrowly misses one of the watercress beds and lurches off through some puddles. The battered car swings out on to the main road and disappears.

I stare at the box, then I pick it up and shake it. It rattles, but only a little.

Dad.

It's from my dad.

My dad the burglar. My dad the thief. The person that no one mentions.

He's been dead for five years.

Ellie and
Uncle Derek

I sit at the bottom of the stairs, staring at Mum's back through the doorway of the living room. I almost call her, but then I look at my name written on top of the box, and I don't.

I could always tell her later.

I can hear Syd dropping cars into the bath. They sound really loud.

Perhaps I *should* tell Mum. She'll be cross that I didn't tell her straight away, but then she'll be weird and moody if I tell her now.

She's funny about dads. She's funny about my dad in particular.

Anyway, it's got my name on it. Not hers.

I pick up the box and carry it up the stairs, to sit on my bed. It fits comfortably on my knees.

The brown parcel tape across the top has one corner that's not quite stuck down.

I wish the man *had* come from Sugar Puffs; this feels like it's going to be complicated. I don't know a lot about Dad, I'm not sure I want to know a lot about Dad, but I'm tingly, my whole body's fizzy. It's as if my blood's turned into fizzy water.

I can't work out if I'm excited, or scared.

Dad?

This came from Dad?

I tug at the tape.

The cardboard flaps spring open, pushed by a mass of balled-up newspaper.

I jump, breathe deeply and straighten out a sheet of newspaper. It's old, but it doesn't say anything special. I feel a slight pang, a dulling. The fizz feels less like tonic water and more like flat cola. But I reach my hand inside.

It closes around something soft, maybe suede? There's metal inside, it clanks. A jewellery case? Perhaps it's a velvet purse full of gold rings and emerald necklaces? Some booty from a long-forgotten heist. I pull it out and run my fingers over it with my eyes closed. No, not jewellery, but a case, holding something metal.

It could still be precious.

I open my eyes. It's brown and oily, not at all like a jewellery case. A leather roll, tied with two long straps. I fumble to undo them, and it tumbles from my hand, falling open across the floor.

Tools?

TOOLS?!?

Just a load of long thin scratchy tools; not a screwdriver in sight.

A lot of rude words go through my head and then I remember what they are.

They're picklocks.

I've seen them before. I close my eyes and I'm back, tiny, so small I can just see over the side of Mum's patchwork quilt. Mum's there, sitting on the bed; she's doing something, maybe brushing her hair?

Dad's there too, his long fingers wrapping the tools, slipping the leather strap around the outside and buckling it closed. I can smell him, something he puts on his hair, or is it his jacket? It's warm and musky.

He picks me up and throws me so I land on the bed and the laughter bursts up from my chest and I reach out for more, but he's leaving again, like he always does.

He smiles at me, his eyes creased and blue and bright before vanishing through the bedroom door. The memory hovers at the side of my head.

The tools feel really big and heavy in my hand, like something that's waiting to be mentioned, something that only grown-ups have, but I know Mum won't like them and she'll take them away from me, so I slip them under the bed.

I reach back into the box and grope about. My fingers pass over some thin bundles of shiny card wrapped in elastic bands, but I grab the largest thing I can find.

Gone with the Wind.

I know this book, it's about a stroppy girl called Scarlett O'Hara. My namesake.

Why on earth would Dad give me that? There's already a copy here, one he gave Mum when I was born.

I reach back into the box and pull out two bundles of photos and postcards.

I peel off the elastic bands. There's one of Mum

looking really young and gorgeous and another of someone who I think is probably Dad, looking sharp. Sideburns and pointy shoes. Some people I don't recognise; some places I've never been to.

The tingly feeling's almost gone away now. There was no golden necklace or emerald ring. I'm back on my bedroom floor with the sound of Syd's cars clanging into the bath.

All I've got is a pile of pictures and a set of tools.

Bing bong.

Maybe the man's back to tell me I *have* won the Sugar Puffs challenge.

I stuff the box under my bed. Syd's on the landing with his arms out, so I pick him up and stumble past the stair gate, letting him clamber backwards down the stairs.

I open the front door.

It's Uncle Derek and Ellie.

Rats. I'd forgotten about Ellie. She's coming to sleep over so that Mum and Uncle Derek can both get to work today. He's on duty now, and Mum's cooking in the care home this evening. Ellie's clutching a big pink flowery duvet, and a white fluffy bear. "Hi, Scarlett," she says.

She's got this drippy voice that always ends on a

low note and she draws smiley faces over her "i"s. I almost can't stand her, but then, nor can anyone else.

"Hi, Ellie. Hi, Uncle Derek," I say, letting them in, forcing myself to smile.

"Morning, Scarlett," says Uncle Derek.

"Oh," calls Mum from the kitchen. "Derek!"

She comes out of the kitchen, wiping her hands on her leggings. She stops in the hall and Uncle Derek pecks her on the cheek. She goes red.

So does he.

He's not really my uncle.

"Oh, Carole, thanks so much, just off to see the new CCTV set-up, in the council offices, yes..." Uncle Derek rubs his chin and twitches in the doorway. He can't stay still. He's a plain-clothes policeman and likes running marathons. I expect he'll run to work today through all the puddles, and then catch a criminal or two and run back with them under his arm. "So, I'll be back at five-fifteen, all right?"

Mum smiles and picks up Syd.

Ellie and I stare at them.

They don't notice us.

Ellie

The thing about policemen, real ones, not the ones in TV detective programmes, is that they're neat. They shine their shoes, they go to work on time and they don't fill the doors of their cars with sausage-roll wrappers. Or at least Ellie's dad doesn't. Actually, he's probably the only policeman I've ever met.

He's very clean and he keeps Ellie clean. Today, she's wearing a blue floral dress with a blue plastic sparkly belt that goes right across the biggest part of her middle.

In spite of the fact that there's a humungous gale

going on out there, she's got spotless white socks.

She's also got thick blue-framed glasses, beaded with raindrops.

I wonder if she can see anything; perhaps she doesn't even know what she looks like in the mirror.

"Shall I put this in Scarlett's room?" she asks Mum, holding up her duvet.

"Of course, Ellie, love," says Mum, glaring at me and pointing up the stairs.

So we go up the stairs, and Ellie puts her duvet on the top bunk, and my room starts to pong of artificial flowers from the washing powder that her dad uses. I almost pull it off and stuff it on the bottom bunk and then I remember that Mum wants me to be nice to Ellie no matter what.

So I don't; I just stick my tongue out at her back instead.

She picks up a pink flowery sweatshirt that I really hate.

"That's nice," she says.

"Yes," I lie.

And there's this oceanic silence between us.

"Pity it's raining," she says.

"Yes," I say, meaning it this time.

I'd hoped we could go swimming in the tank

behind the watercress beds. I love it in there, it's like swimming in an aquarium, but she's so perfectly clean, Ellie would probably see it as freezing cold water buzzing with pond life; I don't think she'd like it somehow. Especially in the rain. Mr Hammond doesn't mind if we swim in the big tank; he says it's fine as long as we don't damage the watercress beds themselves. He likes us living here, we're better than a burglar alarm he says; though how anyone's supposed to steal a load of watercress I can't imagine.

Why they'd do it is even more mysterious.

I look out of the window anyway, in case the sun has changed its mind and stopped sulking.

It hasn't.

Everything outside is grey. Grey concrete around the watercress, the grey tank at the back, the grey landing strip of the airfield next door, the grey control tower.

It's either grey or wet.

Or both.

Neither of us speak. This time I'm sure I can hear the planets rolling across the universe like tumbleweed.

* * *

Downstairs, Mum and Uncle Derek stand out in the rain, talking to each other under an umbrella; Syd's eating two tomatoes at the same time, and I switch on the TV. Ellie follows me. She sits on the sofa at one end of the room, and I sit on the floor at the other end.

We're just in time for *The Numtums*. The screen's full of day-glo dancing squirrels. Syd dances with them, smearing his tomatoey hands over the screen. Perhaps he thinks the squirrels live inside the TV.

There's this annoying little jangly noise, even more annoying than the telly.

Tch, tch, tch, tchty cha, tch, tch, tch. . .

It's Ellie's iPod.

She's lying on her back, pressing buttons on her DS. She's got very big fingers, very big hands. Very big everything, in fact.

She's completely wired up.

I get to my feet, slip out of the door, and slink up to my room. I'll just take a minute, pretend I've been to the bathroom, but I need to have another look in the box.

The first thing I touch is *Gone with the Wind*.

It's yellowed and soft and thumbed. Page thirty-nine is turned down, but there's nothing written on it. I read a few lines, then I sniff the book. It doesn't smell of anything but mouldy bookshelves. There is nothing about this book that says "Dad".

Nothing about the postcards either; they've mostly got Mum's writing on them, with little drawings from me.

They're all addressed to prisons.

I flick through them. There are masses of them. Mostly pictures of Dampington Pier, or the zoo or the town hall. It's as if Mum and I never went anywhere else. I wonder what Dad thought when he got them, I suppose they were pictures of home; although even when he was out of prison, he never ever actually lived with us. He visited quite often, so perhaps he just did short spells behind bars.

I put the cards in date order. The last one was sent in November. He died just before Christmas. There were baubles on the tree in the church, and a knitted nativity scene with a three-legged donkey that I stared at through the whole funeral. I think I thought that if I was really good, and really nice to the plastic baby in the crib, Dad would come back for Christmas.

But he didn't.

Mum collapsed after that. We didn't go out, she just cried all the time and it was the worst Christmas ever.

Soon after, we ended up with Syd's dad, and then Syd. Until Mum and Syd's dad got fed up with each other and she threw him out.

We're not very good at dads in this family.

I push my hands through the crumpled newspaper and feel about inside the box, hoping for something more. The paper rustles as I take out the last few photographs; my fingers touch something small and metal but I can't quite reach it because it's jammed under the cardboard flaps.

I turn the box and slap the underneath with my hand. The metal thing shoots over the carpet.

Ping. It clangs into Syd's tin of cars.

"Oooh," says Ellie, running into the room and picking it up. "Here you are."

I didn't hear her.

Rats. Rats. Rats.

She crouches down next to me and drops it into my hand. It's a key. A tiny poxy key, the sort you use on a rubbish padlock from a cracker.

"I came up to see where you'd gone," she says,

peering into the stuff lying on the floor. "What's this?"

She reaches her pale freckly arm into the balls of newspaper from the top of the box and pulls out a black plastic canister that I hadn't noticed. Before I can stop her, she pops off the top and turns the canister upside down.

A metal roll falls at my feet.

"Oh," says Ellie.

I glare at her.

"I'm only trying to help," she says.

I pick it up and slip off a red elastic band. I hold the roll in my fingers, turning it round and round. It's a little metal film roll, like old-fashioned cameras used. There's a small tab of shiny stuff poking out of the middle between black brushes.

Ellie's got these baby-blue eyes, which look enormous behind her glasses. They're fixed on me now. "What is it?" she asks. "Where did it come from?"

She looks so pathetic I have to tell her.

"But your dad's dead?"

"Yes," I say. "But he left me this lot for when I was eleven. And I am eleven, now."

She gazes at it all.

"What a weird collection of stuff." She picks up *Gone with the Wind* and flicks through it and I have an unreasonable desire to rip it out of her fat fingers. It might be a weird collection of stuff, but it's mine and it was from my dad, not her stinky fabric-conditioned dad, my tough burglar dad.

But I have to be nice to her, for Mum's sake.

I'm so close to tears, I stand up and stare out of the window at Mr Hammond bunching up watercress. There's a big black car out there, and you can tell that it's really clean, because of the way the rain's sliding off it. Right now, I'd like nothing better than a wet walk.

Fat chance.

"Are these all the postcards you and your mum sent him in prison?" Ellie peers at them. "Cute drawings you did, Scarlett."

I turn round, put my hands to the floor and flip my legs up against the top bunk.

"Yes, he must have kept them all," I say between my teeth. "Mum's got a matching set." I try to turn my head towards her, but all the blood's gone to my scalp so it prickles and feels like my eyebrows are going to fall off. Handstands are a good way to stop crying.

"And this?" she says, holding the roll in front of my nose.

"I don't know," I say. I don't want to look. I don't want to hope, because I hate the disappointment.

She shakes it. It doesn't make any noise.

"Well, I'm going to open it," she says, so I crash my legs down to the floor and grab it out of her hands.

In the end both of us open it. She holds one end and I drag the other out across the room. About halfway I have this horrible feeling that it might be an undeveloped film, but within a centimetre or two, it turns to card and then to a long strip of paper.

We spread it across the floor and stare at it.

Keep looking up, Scarlett, keep up the gym, and don't trust just ANYONE.

That's it, that's all it says.

Ellie's big blue eyes blink and stare behind the glasses. Mine almost fill with tears, but I swallow hard, roll the message back inside the container and throw it back in the box.

I do another handstand, and keep doing them until lunchtime.

Doing What Dad Did

I'm lying in bed watching this long shadow stretch across the floor. It's the control tower from the old airfield next door. It means there's a full moon. Ellie's snoring on the top bunk but I'm wide awake.

I'm looking up, at Ellie's mattress above me; I've stuck Dad's message to the underneath of the top bunk.

Keep looking up, Scarlett, keep up the gym, and don't trust just ANYONE.

Useless.

Absolutely useless.

All of it. Even the postcards. They'll mean more

to Mum than to me.

As for telling no one – Ellie already knows.

I turn over and face the wall. I scrunch up my knees and pull the duvet really close.

I try to remember Dad's face, but Ellie's made my bedroom smell funny, so all I can see is her, and her dad. Her bag's like a magic washing-powder stink dispenser, a sort of blue clean smell that smothers everything else. Even Syd's baby wipes. Their whole house pongs of it.

I wonder what ours smells of. Baking? Soup? Poo?

Ellie's is the only house I ever go to these days, and she's the only person that ever comes here. The boys used to; Sam Lewis was round all the time, but he's into football now. The boys at our school have always been more fun than the girls. All the girls are prize horrors and I wouldn't want to bring them home. I certainly wouldn't want to go to their houses, and I'm really glad they never ask me.

I think their mums are scared of us. After all, Dad was a criminal.

But Ellie – honestly, what did I do wrong in a former life to be landed with *her*?

I roll on to my stomach and put my hands

around the bars at the end of the bunk and stare at the wall.

I suppose Ellie's different; she doesn't have any friends, boys or girls, she's only got me because of Uncle Derek and Mum, and we've only got Uncle Derek because he towed out Mum's car when we got stuck in the mud. He's not bothered about Dad, but then he's used to dealing with criminal types.

Although I'm not sure I'd really describe Ellie as a friend.

If she is a friend, she's very annoying.

Are friends supposed to be that irritating?

I turn on to my back, and press my feet up against the underside of Ellie's bunk. I could tip her out.

Or, I could take a look at Dad's tools.

I think of them lying there in the moonlight, waiting for me, only fifteen centimetres away. It's unbearable, so I reach out under the bed for the bundle of picklocks, gently closing my hand around the leather pouch.

I clamber over Ellie's electronic equipment – DS, phone, iPod – all plugged in and glowing in the corner of my bedroom. For a moment I'm tempted to pull out the leads, but I think her gadgets are probably her true friends, and that, although just like Ellie and her dad, they're really annoying, it would be wrong.

Downstairs, Houdini the cat's licking his bottom in the moonlight. He only comes out when Syd's gone to bed.

He breaks off to rub his jaw against my knee. I unroll the tools and he pads over them, making them clink.

"My dad was a burglar, and he's left me his tools," I whisper to Houdini but he just scratches himself on the corner of the sofa.

I run my fingers over the tools. I need to try them. I need to have a go. They're cold and heavy in my hand. I pad through the moonlight into the kitchen. Uncle Derek's parked his running shoes by the back door, next to Mum's wellies. I tiptoe around and pull back the bolt.

Now what?

I stand on the wet gravel. The moon's reflected in the watercress beds. I can hear the stream running into the big tank at the bottom.

The moonlight falls on Mr Hammond's wooden watercress shed. It's got a big padlock dangling from the door and inside there's a locked honesty box, where people pay for the watercress.

The gravel's cold and sharp under my feet, and I try not to let it crunch. An owl hoots off in the trees behind the airfield. Something rustles in the hedge and something else squeals.

I lay Dad's tools on the ground, and choose one of the picks. I've no idea what I'm doing, but I stick the longest in the lock and fiddle about.

Nothing happens.

I take the smallest. Again, nothing happens.

Perhaps this burgling thing is more difficult than it seems.

I try three more before anything feels like it might happen. There's a pick with a thick end. I slip it gently into the padlock, and this time something moves. It's as if my hand holding the padlock can feel the inside, almost as if I can see it. I use my left hand to hold the pick, I don't know why, but it feels right.

Ping. "Yes."

The lock falls open.

It slips off easily, and I lift the door so that it doesn't scrape on the gravel.

This is crazy.

I watch my fingers laying the open padlock on the step.

Mad.

I must be mad.

I stop.

I could just leave.

Or I could go further.

Inside, there's the money box, built into the wall. It's got a different sort of lock. I peer across at it in the gloom.

I should turn round now and lock up the shed.

But instead I reach into the pouch. I pull out a lumpy pick, but it's obviously the wrong thing, so I reach for another set of picks; they're heavier.

Ping.

The tiny door creaks open. I put my hand in and I can feel notes; masses of pound coins. Real money. But I like Mr Hammond and I don't think Dad would have stolen from him. It feels wrong, so I won't touch anything.

But now I know that I could be…

…I could be a burglar too.

My Big Mistake

Monday morning.

Nearly five o'clock.

I think I've been awake all night. Ellie went home yesterday and my room smells almost normal again. I've done nothing about Dad's box, except hang the poxy key around my neck on an orange shoelace and wonder why he gave it to me now.

I imagine, Dad was trying to tell me something. But I can't see what. It feels like it's all a big clue to something. But I can't work it out. Perhaps he should have waited until I was older; I might have been cleverer.

He left me his tools, so he must have wanted me to break into things. So I will, and I'll do it properly. I've been thinking about the equivalent of a jewel robbery in Dampington, and I think I've come up with exactly the right target.

A mission.

Downstairs, Houdini looks hopeful, so I feed him. Then, tucking the roll of picklocks under my arm, I slip out.

There are no cars. No one's up, but it's nearly light out here and the birds think it's morning. The grass is wet under my feet, and nettles brush my legs as I take the footpath past the airfield into town.

This feels like a dream, I can't possibly be doing it in real life.

My spine's tingling. My blood's turned back to fizz again. I have to stop and breathe for a minute, because part of me feels like I could explode.

"Hey!" I shout at the fields. A single crow takes off from a phone line and flaps off, creaking and screeching.

"HEY!"

I wait.

This time, nothing moves. There was only me and the crow, and now he's gone.

I walk on. I keep thinking of Dad. I'm doing what he did. I'm on a job, an early morning visit to a rich person's house, to relieve them of unwanted jewellery. In order to succeed, I must move like a wraith through the town. No one must ever know I've been here – even a footprint could land me in it.

When I reach Dampmouth Bay, I slip down a side alley and stay absolutely still. The streets are empty. There are noises down in the harbour, but nothing up here in the town.

I stay there waiting for the longest possible time, listening to myself breathing in and out, in and out.

I could just go home.

Abandon the whole thing.

But I don't.

I walk a little further.

Just off the high street is Ye Olde Sweete 'n' Toys Shoppe. One window's crammed with jars and lollipops and tins of stripy candy. The other, Nerf guns, Lego and Playmobil.

I stand to one side as if I just happen to be there,

waiting by the wall for a lift at five-thirty in the morning.

Listening, I can't hear anyone around, no footsteps, no cars, but I think up an excuse. *"I was window shopping, it's my brother's birthday."*

Not great, but it'll do if anyone appears now, this second. I put my hand on the doorknob, slip one of the picks into the lock and I don't even stop to think what I'm doing.

Clunk, clunk, clunk.

Nothing happens.

A tiny pulse of panic starts on the side of my head. Bet this never happened to Dad.

I pull out the longest pick.

Clunk, clunk, ping.

I turn the knob and the door opens a crack.

If an alarm goes off, I'm dead. I hold my breath for at least a minute, but nothing happens, the shop just breathes out at me, hotly, fruitily, beckoning me inside.

Yes!

Yes. Yes.

I've done it. I've opened the door to the most exciting shop in town.

For a moment I'm awed by my own ability, then I

remember that I've been standing here for possibly five whole minutes, and that anyone could have spotted me. A sudden wriggle of fear shoots down my back and I turn, almost expecting someone to be there, watching me. But all's still, so I step over the threshold.

I push the door shut and stare. Every sort of sweet I could possibly want is there right in front of me, and I can take as much as I like. The jars line the walls, prices written on in felt tip; the top of the counter's scattered with baskets of wrapped sweets and underneath those are rows of brightly coloured boxes crammed with more sweets.

I check behind the counter, just in case someone's hiding there, but of course they're not and no little red lights are flashing. On the other hand, I should make it quick, in case there's some sort of secret alarm and the police arrive.

I look up at the jars lining the walls.

I'm frozen, paralysed by the possibilities, but then I remember my mission – a prize from each part of the shop.

I'm tempted to take a whole box of fizzing snakes, but they'd be missed and I'd have to explain them away at home so instead I stuff two fizzing snakes in my mouth and feel the popping candy explode up my nose.

Delicious.

I stuff two more in my pocket and grab ten bubblegums. Then I take down the jar of sherbet raspberries, weigh out exactly two hundred grams and tip them into a paper bag.

That's enough.

But I spot a bag of liquorice whirls and stuff that in my pocket too.

Definitely enough.

I pop one more fizzing snake in my mouth and move on to the toy shop behind. One side is heaped with boxes of spangly pink dolls, horses and teddies, the kind of thing Ellie likes. The other side has the boy stuff. I run my fingers over the wheels of a skateboard; I'd like a skateboard but there's no way I'd get away with it. Mum would find it and kill me, slowly.

I crouch down to look at the shelves of toys for little kids. The dinosaurs are fun, but Syd doesn't really need any more of them. I trail past the trains, and tractors and cars. At the end there's a display of Lego wind-up torches. They're little Lego people but big, and turned into torches. So I help myself to a policeman.

Perhaps I'll give it to Uncle Derek for Christmas.

I really don't think there's anything else I could possibly want; anyway, I need to get out.

Back on the street, it's full daylight. My pockets are bursting and I'd quite like breakfast.

Bong, bong, bong, bong, bong, bong.

Six o'clock.

Syd'll be awake, which means Mum'll be awake.

I try and relock the door, but I can't. I try again, but I haven't a clue how to do it. I just pull it shut. It doesn't even do that properly.

Bet that never happened to Dad, either.

A car drives past the end of the alley, pauses, and drives on. A dustbin lorry rattles down the high street.

A tractor engine starts up somewhere out of town.

I turn my back on the shop and run.

Ecology

Dampmouth Bay Zoo is about as exciting as the watercress beds. The only things that are any good are the butterfly house and the souvenirs. The whole class stares longingly at the gift shop while Mrs Gayton hands out clipboards.

I can hardly keep my eyes open but I stick one hand out for a clipboard while selecting a sherbet raspberry from my pocket with the other. Mrs Gayton ignores me and hands a clipboard to Melissa instead.

"Ecology, Golden Class," says Mrs Gayton. "That's the purpose of our visit."

I don't think this zoo is very ecological. It's not very eco and it's not logical either. Some tired monkeys hang from the roof in their small stinky cage and there's an anteater that refuses to come out. He seems to have a room the size of a swimming pool. There are also two tired flamingos that haven't eaten enough prawns and seem to be turning grey.

And a lot of concrete.

Like the watercress beds, but I suspect the watercress beds have more ecology going on.

I've only brought the sherbet raspberries, and two bubblegums, and I feel weird. One moment, I feel fantastic, like I know something that no one else knows. Then I feel slightly sick.

It could just be lack of sleep.

I'm with Ellie. Of course I'm with Ellie, I'm the only person that isn't mean to her. Melissa, Jessica and Amber are already giggling behind their hands. Of all the horrible girls in our class, those three are the worst. Mum calls them the Coven. It helps, because that way I can always think of them as witches who will ultimately come to a bad end if they keep it up. They're giggling at Ellie because of her clothes, which is almost fair enough as Ellie's clothes are never good, but today they're epically misjudged. Pink fluffy jumper, oversized backpack, tight pink leggings that make her legs look like cocktail sausages and spangly see-through boots.

Oh, and she's wearing a hat.

No one ever wears a hat, even though it's always on the list that Mrs Gayton sends out. I bet, even though it's raining, she's got the suntan lotion too.

"Now, Golden Class, take your clipboards and answer as many questions as possible; if you get stuck, you're obviously not trying hard enough."

Mrs Gayton heads off to the café. She's probably hoping that someone will be eaten by the lion or savaged by the mangy tiger. I expect she'd really love it if it was me or Ellie.

Mrs Gayton's part of the reason why Ellie and I manage to get on. She's evil to both of us: Ellie's clever and Mrs Gayton hates clever people, they show her up. I'm the daughter of a thief, and she never lets me forget it. She always holds her handbag close when I'm near, as if I'm going to steal it from round her arm. She's about 108. She's been at the school since Mum was there and I think Mrs Mason, the head teacher, is too scared to sack her.

Mrs Gayton actually seems to like the Coven; perhaps she recognises something of herself in them.

We leave the boys trying to tempt the anteater out with a chocolate brownie and I push open the flappy door that leads to the butterflies. It's absolutely boiling and a little creepy. These huge butterflies flap slowly over our heads. They mostly look fairly tatty, like old curtains.

I offer Ellie the little paper bag of sherbets. "Oh – thanks, Scarlett." She pops one in her mouth. It matches her hat.

I take one myself and push it round my mouth. I should be massively enjoying it, but somehow, it doesn't taste so good. I feel slightly better that Ellie's eaten one too, it spreads the guilt, although strictly speaking she doesn't know it's stolen, so she can't feel guilty.

Was Dad wracked with guilt every time he committed a burglary?

"Ellie, have you ever done anything really wrong?" I ask, pretending to look at a brown moth. It's probably dead, or maybe it's a piece of bark.

"Wrong?" asks Ellie. "What d'you mean?"

"I mean, like stealing? For example?"

Ellie's peering at a rock. I think it's actually a frog, but Ellie's short-sighted, so it comes as a surprise to her when it gets up and walks over the mossy stones. "Are you thinking about your dad?"

I wasn't, but I'm scared of what she's going to say if I tell her the truth, and nod my head.

"Well, I'm sure, even with your dad, there were grey areas." We move along as a man in a suit and a chauffeur's hat shuffles through the plastic flaps and gazes around. A large blonde woman in a leopard-skin coat squeezes in behind him, and I could swear she stares at me more than the butterflies.

"That's the lady mayoress," says Ellie, pointing backwards.

I look again at the large woman. She's wearing a huge golden chain, but because of her fur coat, I can barely see it. What on earth is she doing in the butterfly house?

"Lady mayoress?" I ask. "Surely not, she looks like..." I can't think of anything polite.

"A Christmas decoration?" asks Ellie. "Don't you remember, she won the election last summer? Dad said it was a surprise; they've only been living here three years. She brought the chauffeur with her."

I stare at them. The chauffeur looks like the sort

of man that hangs out outside the betting shop; his grey suit's all rumpled, and his hair's too long.

"You mean they run the council?" I mutter.

"Yes," whispers Ellie. "Dad says her election was iffy, he thinks they rigged the vote, but no one can prove it now."

Trust Ellie to know something like that. I shrug and lead her further through from Africa to South America.

"Anyway, thing is," she says, "it all depends on what you steal, and why. It's a bit like white lies."

"So you're saying that sometimes it's OK to steal?"

"Yes. And no. I mean, we don't really know the details of what your dad stole, and from whom."

Only Ellie would say "whom".

"Right," I say. I kick at a mushroom thing growing out of a log. It oozes yellow pus-like stuff all over my shoe. Serves me right for stealing sweets. "But, it wasn't really about Dad."

"Oh?" says Ellie, pushing through the plastic flaps at the other end of the butterfly house. "What did you...?"

But she stops in the middle of the sentence.

We're standing at the back of the zoo, the air

suddenly damp and fresh on our faces. In front of us, there's this tiny concrete pond with three penguins squeezed into it. They look deeply, deeply sad.

They've always looked quite sad, but they used to have a bigger pond; I'm sure they did. Now the concrete seems to have been nibbled away around the edges and they've only got about a foot of water.

Luckily it's raining, otherwise they'd never be able to get completely wet.

We both stand and stare.

"Oh no, it's like they're in prison," says Ellie.

Mrs Gayton joins us by the rail. "Just like your father was," she says to me. "The difference is that the penguins don't deserve it."

I swallow and slip along the rail as far from her as possible.

"Nasty," says Ellie.

"Yes," I murmur. "Shame it's not her in there."

We walk right around the penguins' enclosure. It's tiny, smaller than our sitting room.

"This is awful," I murmur to Ellie.

"This is really wrong," she says.

"We should do something about it," I say.

"Yes," says Ellie doubtfully. "But what?"

Toy Story vs
Uncle Derek

By the evening, I'm sick with nerves about the sweets. Like father like daughter, two happy thieves together, all in a thieves' den. Perhaps Mum's a burglar too? I could really do with an evening with Mum on the sofa, watching one of her soppy movies, eating peanut-butter sandwiches and drinking banana milkshakes, but instead it's going to be Uncle Derek and Ellie.

Mum and Uncle Derek have swapped. She's gone to work and he's come back to look after us.

"Look after" is a bit of an exaggeration. He's come back to burn some sausages and have a scrap with Syd in the bathroom while they blacken.

They're still up there. I can hear Syd fighting back. He's already employed ordinary tools of warfare, now I imagine he's entering the Roman phase. They used dead cows and balls of fire in their catapults. Syd makes do with bubble bath and the sink plunger. It has a similar effect, because Uncle Derek gives up and lets Syd out of the bath.

Syd can be quite feisty when it comes to Uncle Derek.

"Mrs Gayton was horrid again today," says Ellie, over the burnt sausages.

"Hm?" says Uncle Derek; he's stuffing potato in Syd's mouth.

"Yes," says Ellie. "How do you stand it, Scarlett? She's vile about your dad."

I shrug and fill my mouth with peas. It's kind of nice of her to say it, but I also wish she wouldn't.

"Is she?" asks Uncle Derek, looking right at me. "Does she do it often?"

I can't answer, I'd cry if I did. I look back at my plate and make a face from the sausages. There's nothing else to do with them.

When Syd's finally gone to bed, Uncle Derek joins

us in front of the telly. We've been watching *Toy Story 3* for the six millionth time, but as he won't let us watch anything that isn't a U or a PG, it's a choice of that or *Barbie on Ice*. At least, I'm watching it; Ellie's on her DS.

On the screen, the toys have made their escape but they're on the conveyor belt slipping down towards the rubbish. Here in the sitting room, Uncle Derek's next to us, running on the spot with a stopwatch. I notice he's growing a moustache. I think he thinks it makes him look cool. Actually, it just makes him look like a man who can't grow a moustache properly.

"Twenty-one, twenty-two, twenty-three," he pants.

The toys tip into the rubbish chute.

Uncle Derek stops and takes his pulse. "Fifty-five, fifty-six."

The toys clutch each other and sink towards the furnace in the middle.

Uncle Derek runs again.

The toys say their goodbyes – this is the bit where Mum starts crying if she's here.

"Thirty-nine, forty, forty-one – hurgh." Uncle Derek falls back on an armchair. "All done."

The plastic aliens rescue the toys with the claw. I don't really know what he's "all done", but I'm glad it's over.

Uncle Derek is really quite annoying; I don't mind him as a babysitter, but beyond that...

I get about a minute's peace while Uncle Derek "tests his recovery rate", and I'm sucked back into the story.

The toys are on their way back home, it's all going to be all right.

"Blimey!" says Uncle Derek, leaping to his feet.

I stare at the screen, I was really hoping we could get to the end of the movie without more Uncle Derek fuss, but he's really jumping about this time.

Ellie even looks up from the DS.

"Where did these come from?" He's looking in my school bag.

"Dad," says Ellie. "What're you doing?"

"These." Uncle Derek holds up the roll of tools.

"What are they?" asks Ellie.

They both stare at me.

Rats. I left the top open.

I stare at the telly, but I can feel the blush creeping down from my hairline.

"Dad's," I mutter.

"Yes – I guessed that – but did your mum have them all this time?" Uncle Derek looks worried, so I take a long time to answer.

"No, Dad's solicitor brought them."

"But what are they?" asks Ellie, again.

Uncle Derek looks at me really hard. "Does your mum know?"

I shrug. I'm not going to tell him, it's none of his business.

"Oh." He places the roll of tools on the arm of the chair and sits back.

We all stare at them, except for Woody and Buzz, who are climbing in and out of cardboard boxes on the screen.

Uncle Derek's face is mostly white, with two little pink spots on his cheeks.

"D'you know what they're for?" he asks.

I turn my head back to the screen. Perhaps he'll just go away if I don't show any interest.

Really slowly, he unrolls the tools so that they lie glinting on the floor. I look at them again. Long slender picks, with hooked pointy ends. He reaches into a pocket at the back of the pouch, and pulls out a key. Well, a sort of key. The end looks like a key, but the rest of it's more like a saw. I'd never noticed that one.

"A bump key," he says, pulling out the longest of the tools in the pouch. "And this thing here is an overlifter, very handy on mortice locks."

"What are you talking about?" asks Ellie, looking across between me and her dad.

Uncle Derek's face moves through panic, confusion, sadness and lands in exhaustion. He looks at his watch. "What time's your mum due back?"

Uncle Derek
Spills the Beans

We're still sitting on the sofa with the tools laid out in front of us. Uncle Derek tried to offer us another film, a 12 this time, but Ellie wasn't going to be bought off that easily. I really want him to go away but he can't sit down now, it's like he's got popping candy in his pants. He keeps clicking the top of his stopwatch, in, out, in, out, in, out. "What d'you know about your dad, Scarlett?" He jogs from one foot to the other.

"He went to prison," I mutter.

"That's it? That's all you know? You've never been told anything else, by anyone? Not even your mum? So you've just grown up thinking your dad was a criminal?"

I nod.

"Oh – that's fine, then," he says.

What's he getting at?

"Well – she has told me other things," I say, trying to sound cautious and knowing at the same time.

"Like?" he asks.

I nod towards Ellie, as if there's some huge secret I know but that she shouldn't, and comb the past for any scrap that might make Uncle Derek think I know everything about Dad. What has Mum told me? "She's told me he wasn't all bad, that he didn't *just* burgle…" I say it as significantly as I can.

"OK, fine." He sits back in the chair.

There's a silence while Uncle Derek clicks his stopwatch again. Did he believe me? I gaze at my fingernails, waiting.

"So are these something to do with being a burglar?" Ellie asks, prodding the tools.

Uncle Derek nods. "Yes, love, they're for lock-picking. Scarlett's dad probably had several sets. They were the tools of his trade. Sort of."

"What do you mean — sort of?" asks Ellie.

"Nothing — nothing — I was just surprised to see them there — that's all." But I can see he's got something else he's dying to say.

I stare at the rug to stop myself speaking. I do the full-on stare, the one that would melt steel if the rug was made of steel. It helps. I manage not to say anything.

"Well, there *is* another little thing, Ellie; but wouldn't you rather wait until your mum gets back, Scarlett?"

I shake my head. Ellie shakes hers. "It's fine, you can say it in front of Ellie," I say, still giving the rug my full attention. Uncle Derek may be really annoying, but just this once, I'm ready to listen to him. He might actually be about to tell me something interesting about my dad.

He doesn't speak, so I risk looking up. He's dangling by his fingernails from the door frame. "Really?" he says.

I nod.

"Come on, Dad," says Ellie. "I want to know what Scarlett knows, what you know."

Uncle Derek rubs his hands over his belly, only he hasn't got a belly, he's got a toast rack. He's looking at his stopwatch again. Perhaps he's timing the conversation.

He sits down. "So your mum's told you everything, then?" he says.

I try to look bored. I daren't speak in case I say the wrong thing, so instead, I heave a long sigh.

"Did her dad do something really awful?" asks Ellie. "Like murder someone?"

Uncle Derek's head whips round to look at Ellie. "NO – nothing like that. Quite the opposite, actually. He saved lives, all over the place."

Saved lives?

I say nothing and keep staring at the pattern on the rug. I can feel my ears turning red.

"How come?" says Ellie.

I shrug. "You can tell her," I say, struggling to keep the excitement out of my voice.

"Have you ever heard of the Official Secrets Act, Ellie, love?"

"Isn't it about keeping quiet about government things?"

Uncle Derek sighs. "Loosely, yes. It means that years after something has happened that the government might want to keep secret, lots of people that worked for the government or who lived with people who worked for the government are bound to silence." He looks at me. "Scarlett's mum's one of them."

"Are you?" asks Ellie.

Uncle Derek screws up his face. "Sort of."

I glance up from the rug. Ellie's staring at her dad.

"So what did Scarlett's dad do? Work for the government?"

Uncle Derek nods. "Very much so."

"So why did they put him in prison?" asks Ellie.

"They didn't," says Uncle Derek, staring at the rug, probably at the same spot as me. "He was on top-secret missions, all over the world. He needed a cover. Prison was perfect. They kept an imaginary 'Quick' Dick McNally in solitary confinement, so that he could spy for them."

Ellie lets out a squeak. I can't make any noise at all but I stand up, as if my legs want to leave the room.

"So yes, he stole things, but he wasn't an ordinary, run-of-the-mill housebreaker. He stole for the government. He stole secrets. He ... repatriated things. He was a secret-agent burglar, if you like. And Scarlett's mum knew, but she's not allowed to tell anyone, even now, because she'd be breaking the Official Secrets Act."

I sit back down, or rather, my legs fold.

"So how come she told Scarlett?" asks Ellie.

I freeze, waiting for Uncle Derek to ask me, but he doesn't. "He was Scarlett's dad, it's fair enough." Uncle Derek turns to me. "How long ago did she tell you?"

I take a deep breath but Ellie cuts in. "So what was all that about him being a jewel thief?" she asks.

"Well, he might have started off that way – but essentially, he was an international safe-cracker, a very good one, and once he started to work for the government, he wasn't even outside the law..."

I reach for a picture of Dad that Mum's put on the piano. There he sits, smiling, relaxed, lolling. He looks kind of ordinary.

A spy?

Today is getting really weird.

"So how do *you* know?" Ellie says, asking the question that's on the tip of my tongue.

Uncle Derek clicks the stopwatch about five million times. "I've – worked it out, sort of, and things, you know, at work. This and that."

This time I stare at him.

"I don't believe you," says Ellie. "If everyone's signed the Official Secrets Act, then no one would tell you anything, unless you were supposed to know."

Uncle Derek flushes a deep beetroot. "He's always been a part of my job," he says to the rug.

"What part?" I ask, remembering how Uncle Derek turned up so suddenly the day we first met him, the day we broke down; and how quickly he came round to tea, trailing Ellie behind him.

"He was on my patch, I had to know," says Uncle Derek. "I needed to know that he wasn't just a jewel thief, that he was really a spy, otherwise when there was a burglary roundabouts, I'd have been knocking on Carole's door instead of finding the real criminal." Uncle Derek looks quite pleased with his explanation.

"Crikey," says Ellie.

Uncle Derek's talking again. "And — of course, there were enemies."

Ellie's eyes widen. "International spies?"

"Not spies so much as gangsters, and not all that international. Some of his jobs were here in Britain, and he upset some nasty characters on the way past." Uncle Derek takes a deep breath. "Spying isn't all about the government. Some of it's to do with uncovering corruption, and thwarting out-and-out lawbreaking. There was a big jewellery heist in South London; Dick McNally took the jewels back from under the thieves' noses."

Uncle Derek stands up and throws a couple of punches into the air, as if downing an invisible criminal. "The Queenie Gang, they were called. They didn't like it. There were a lot of threats after that. As a policeman, I needed to be on the lookout. Dick McNally was always vulnerable, they all knew about him, and we needed to keep you and your mum secret," he says, looking at me.

"Ooo," says Ellie. "You mean someone might have been after Scarlett because of her dad?"

"Yes," says Uncle Derek. "But not any more, that's all in the past. Though it's odd that the solicitor brought you the tools now. Was there anything else with them?"

I stare at Ellie. "No," I say.

It's Ellie's turn to stare at the rug. I don't think she likes lying.

"It's only that it's rumoured that Dick McNally was always paid in diamonds."

"Why paid in diamonds?" I ask.

Uncle Derek raises an eyebrow. "You didn't know that?"

"I didn't," I say quite truthfully.

"Oh," says Uncle Derek quietly. He sighs. "If it's true, which it probably isn't, maybe he was putting them away for a rainy day. They're smaller than gold, and safer than bank accounts. And they're international. As it is, the rainy day came before he told anyone where they were. Or if they really existed."

We sit watching the blank screen of the TV thinking about imaginary diamonds that were never found.

"How did he die?" asks Ellie.

Uncle Derek looks up at me.

"He went over a cliff," I say. "They said he was going too fast. His hands slipped on the wheel." I shrug.

"He was being chased," says Uncle Derek quietly. "Someone was after him, witnesses saw it, and at the last minute, he swerved and drove himself over the edge."

My spine prickles.

"On purpose?" asks Ellie.

"Who knows," says Uncle Derek, checking his watch for the millionth time. "Now I've already told you too much. Off you go, bedtime."

Sherbet Raspberries
Aren't Always Nice

"Diamonds. Did he say diamonds?" asks Ellie.

"Yes," I say. "He did. But it was only a rumour, remember – they can't possibly exist."

"*Did* you know all that about your dad?"

I stare at the underneath of Ellie's bunk. "No, and I don't think he was supposed to tell us."

"Probably not," says Ellie. "But it's not your fault, you didn't really lie to him, did you? I mean, he just walked into it."

"Yes," I say, not really listening. I'm thinking about Dad. So he wasn't in prison, he was off on highly secret missions. Prison was just a cover when he was really clambering in through embassy windows to "liberate" documents. He wasn't actually a burglar.

And he didn't steal jewels, he was paid in them.

So he was honest.

Yeah! My dad was honest.

He wasn't a thief, he was a hero — sort of.

He should be celebrated, not swept under the carpet.

I wind up the policeman torch and point it at the underside of Ellie's mattress.

Keep looking up, Scarlett, keep up the gym, and don't trust just ANYONE.

He was a good man, my dad.

I shine the torch across the room at the little disco ball that hangs in my window. It twists in the breeze and shards of light sparkle on the walls.

I roll over and stick a sherbet raspberry in my mouth. It tastes disgusting with toothpaste but still does the fizzing thing on my tongue. I turn it over and over until a small hole becomes a big hole and I have to crunch down on it, smashing the shell into sticky shards that glue to my teeth.

I should really have enjoyed that, but I didn't because I've jumped to the wrong conclusion. I thought that because Dad was a thief, coming from a long line of thieves, he wanted me to be one too. But he can't possibly have done.

Stupid me.

Stupid, stupid, stupid me.

Now what?

The box. It must be about something else, not thieving, but finding. Do I just need to find where the key fits? Is it as simple as that?

I feel the key round my neck. A key is an honest way of getting into things.

I remember the moment when I broke into the shop and squirm.

I got it completely wrong.

Everyone's got it completely wrong. All those people, and I'm thinking particularly of Mrs Gayton, who's always said that Dad was a thief, are wrong too.

But I can't tell them the truth, because of the Official Secrets thingy, and anyway, it's bound to come back to Mum, and Uncle Derek shouldn't have told us anyway, because he's signed it.

Rats.

I swing the torch across the ceiling; the light catches Ellie's hand dangling from the top bunk.

She knows the truth, she knows, and her dad knows that my dad was a good man. Although she's fantastically annoying with all her jangly little machines and their pingy music, she's always been truthful. Always been kind. Perhaps I can try to do the same.

Maybe, from now on, I can try to be honest, and do what Dad really wanted. I can help other people, and use the picklocks in a positive way.

If I've got the courage.

Confession

"You didn't. That's awful." Ellie's baby-blue eyes are wider than I've ever seen them.

I nod my head and feel sick again. Saying it out loud is the worst thing, that's probably why it's taken me three days to confess.

"I thought you were being weird because of your dad, not because you've been..." She can't actually say *stealing*. "But, Scarlett, that's criminal."

"I know," I say, washing my hands for the millionth time.

"But whatever possessed you? You complete ... idiot!"

"I know." I try to find a bit of towel to dry my hands that isn't completely disgusting.

Clangalangalangalangalang.

The end of dinner. Time to come out from our hiding place in the toilets. We walk into class.

"Whatever happens, they'll send you to prison."

"What?"

"Yes — ten is the age of criminal responsibility, once you're ten, you can be locked up."

"Really?"

"There's this thing," says Ellie, "called the boot."

"The boot?" I ask.

"Yes, they put your foot in this metal boot, fill it with sawdust and pour water on it."

The Coven close in on our left.

"In the end, your foot falls off and you die of blood poisoning," says Ellie.

"In prison, now?"

"No — in the fifteenth century, probably."

"Right, class, sit quietly now." No one pays any attention to Mrs Gayton, who sits with a sucked-lemon expression on her face at the front of the room.

When she pinches in her cheeks, all the hairs on her chin stick up and she looks more like a potato than a teacher.

I don't think she's really a Mrs Gayton, I think she's really a Mr. There isn't an ounce of girliness in her. Perhaps she's really a potato.

I stare at her chin. There are more hairs than ever.

She's been teaching since the last century; or not teaching. I've certainly never learned anything.

The gnarled fingers of her left hand drum on the desk. With her right, she holds a biro and squeezes the life out of it.

I wonder if she's ever stolen anything. She's certainly confiscated loads of things; none of them ever come back. Is that stealing? They haven't locked her up, yet.

Ellie, of course, sits down right at the front and gazes up at Mrs Gayton's potato face. I find a chair near the back, with the boys. Sam Lewis budges up so that I can sit next to him. The Coven settle in right behind Ellie and snigger. I can see her stiffen, but she won't say anything back to them, she never does, and Mrs Gayton says bullying doesn't exist.

That's because Mrs Gayton models herself on teachers from Mars. She certainly doesn't model herself on teachers from Earth. I'm sure teachers are supposed to listen to children and teach by example.

I'd sit at the front with Ellie, but I never know the answers to anything, so I feel safer here with the boys. I bet most of them have stolen something. In fact, I'm sure Sam Lewis got caught pinching crisps from the Grocery Basket last year and he's not in prison. He looks rather happy.

I stare out of the window. If Ellie's wrong and I don't go to prison, I need to do the right thing. Even if Ellie's right, and I do go to prison, I need to do the right thing. I need to use Dad's picklocks to make the world a better place.

The light catches raindrops on the window.

Diamonds.

I stroke the little key around my neck, it looks like it would open a musical instrument case or a briefcase.

We haven't got any musical instruments at home.

Or any briefcases.

And *Gone with the Wind*? What's that supposed to tell me?

I will stop thinking about the diamonds as they almost certainly don't exist and if they ever did, they're at the bottom of the North Sea with Dad.

After about a century, everyone goes kind of quiet. Mrs Gayton's practically sucked her lips inside her head and has to do a gurn before she can even speak.

"Ecology, Golden Class, what does it mean?"

Ellie's hand shoots up. "Miss, Miss."

No one else even moves. Mrs Gayton's lip curls as she runs her gaze over the whole class.

Ellie's going to pop in a minute and the Coven are in stitches watching her. So is everyone else. The boys sitting next to me, who never normally notice anything, start to giggle.

Eventually, without looking at her, Mrs Gayton sighs. "Ellie, give us your pearls of wisdom."

"Ecology, miss, is the relationship between a creature or plant and its environment."

Mrs Gayton nods. "Almost. It's the *study* of the relationship between the living organism and its environment."

Melissa, top witch, wrinkles up her nose and sticks it in the air, pointing her fingers at Ellie's back.

"Now, Golden Class, *if* you're capable of it, I want you to think about the creatures you saw in the excellent zoo on Monday, and the environments they come from. What, for example, makes a flamingo pink?"

I think of the penguins in their sad concrete home, "SEALIFE CENTRE" written over the doorway into their hut in cracked blue lettering painted on to the brown pebble-dash. Ellie called it a prison. Could I live the rest of my life in somewhere like that?

I'd have to sleep on a concrete bench that smelled of fish.

I imagine Mrs Gayton throwing me sardines from a bucket.

I hate sardines.

What were the zoo keepers thinking when they put them in there? I can't believe it's very like the Arctic, or is it the Antarctic? I start to think myself into the cold. I'm imagining the ice and snow of a huge white empty freezing space, and I'm whizzing over the top of it, like one of those helicopter-mounted wildlife cameras, skimming over the icebergs till I find happy penguins plunging off the ice floes into the clear turquoise waters.

I draw the three penguins diving into the iceberg water.

They're wearing diamond necklaces.

And then I rub them out.

Mrs Gayton views drawing as a weakness, it's a sign of thought, and Mrs Gayton doesn't like thought.

Also, the diamonds are just a rumour.

"Ellie!"

I look up. Ellie's twitching around in the front of the class, trying to reach down her back. "I'm sorry, miss, but..."

The Coven's hooting wildly, and Mrs Gayton's sucked her cheeks back in, glaring at Ellie. I can't see what's happening, but something's really wrong.

Mrs Gayton stands, boiling with fury. "Ellie! Out — recover yourself." She stomps to the door and opens it. "Out! Now!"

Ellie stumbles to the door, both her hands stuck down the back of her neck, slapping at her sweatshirt. Her head's twisted round as far as it will go, but judging by the expression on her face, she still can't see what's driving her mad. It does look ridiculous, and behind her the whole class explodes with laughter.

Blackjacks Only
Come in Sixes

"Earwigs," says Ellie.

"Earwigs?"

"Yes — when I got to the toilets I took my top off and a load of earwigs fell out."

"Yuk," I say, pulling our front door closed.

"Exactly, yuk." Ellie holds the gate open for me and we set off for town across the fields. It's stopped raining now, but the hedgerows drip, and the path's got thin mud on it.

"So that's what Melissa was doing — putting earwigs down your back." With every step I feel crosser on Ellie's behalf. I also feel cross with myself for keeping silent. I knew there was something wrong, but I just sat there watching. "You should tell Mrs Gayton, or Mrs Mason," I say. "I should tell Mrs Mason."

Ellie turns her big blue glasses on me. "No — please don't, I don't want to go there."

"But, Ellie? It's wrong."

Ellie shakes her head. "It's silly, they'll grow out of it. They'll stop soon."

I climb over the stile. Ellie follows.

"That's your dad talking, but I bet *he* wouldn't just let it happen to *him*."

She turns to face me; I can see the tears bursting up behind her eyes. "Scarlett, if you tell anyone, anyone at all, I'll never be your friend again."

I stare at her. For a moment, I'm speechless. Never be *my* friend. I thought *I* was the one befriending *her*. And then I think of it from her point of view. "OK, I won't, I promise."

"Good. Now, let's take those things back to the shop."

Ellie's convinced that if I give all the stuff back, I'll stop feeling ill. I suggested posting it, or stuffing it through the letter box after closing, but she stared at me through her glasses until I agreed. We went home on the school bus and now I've got it all jammed inside my coat, except for the sherbet raspberries; there's only one left and we've decided I won't go to prison for that.

The thing is, it's not that easy to return things to a shop without being spotted.

Especially when the shop turns out to be completely empty, and the woman behind the counter glares at you like you might be about to steal something.

"Can I help you?" The woman stares at us over her glasses. She looks like a close relative of Mrs Gayton's. She probably is and probably hates me already.

Ellie freezes. I'm desperate to freeze but have a brilliant idea and fumble for my pocket money.

I look for the tallest jar. "Some fruit pips, please?"

"A hundred grams?" The woman checks me over her glasses, again, and turns to the shelves behind her. It only takes her a second to stand on a stool to get the fruit pips and she's pouring them out on to the scales.

"Blackjacks?" I say, looking for the lowest sweets.

"How many?" She whips round and replaces one

jar while getting the next.

"Ten?" I say.

"I only sell them in sixes."

"OK – twelve then."

She starts counting them out.

I haven't been able to put anything back, although the bubblegums are now in my hand, waiting to be dropped into their basket.

"Anything else?"

My eyes race over the shelves. Some of the jars look heavier than others, they might be harder to move. "Blue bubble chews? Six, please?"

The woman turns round, hands on her hips. "Those come in fours." She jabs a finger at the jar. "See?"

"Eight, then, please."

The woman takes out eight sweets. But she's facing me the whole time.

Ellie drops two pounds into my hand. "Gobstoppers?" she says, pointing to a box under the counter.

"Three small gobstoppers?"

"I only sell them in fives."

The woman gets down on her hands and knees to pull the box out of the drawer.

It gives me time to dump the bubblegums.

We spend almost our entire pocket money in her shop. We end up with gobstoppers, fruit pips, blue bubble chews, flying saucers and humbugs. I hate humbugs, but they were the best because they were all stuck together in the jar and it took the woman ages to separate them. She had to get a knife from the back room.

We step back on to the pavement, our pockets full of legal sweets. Ellie's right, I do feel better, not only have I put everything, nearly everything, back, but I've spent more money than I ate.

Ellie sticks a gobstopper in her mouth. "Where did you put the Lego torch?"

"In the Barbie display," I say.

Ellie laughs and nearly chokes.

We swing out of the alley, carefree and loaded down with sugar. I've replaced the sweets, paid back the shop, and best of all, even if I can't tell anyone, I know my dad wasn't really a burglar, he was really a hero. Sort of. He did good things, and I've started to do good things too, now.

And good things make you feel good.

That must be why Dad changed from being a

burglar to being a spy.

He was more like Ellie's dad than someone that Ellie's dad would lock up.

We would just walk on the road, but we have to climb up on to the high pavement to get past the mayoress's car. I can tell it's hers because it's got a tiny flag on the front.

"What a funny place to park," says Ellie, stopping to examine the tax disc. "And it's out of date."

I stop to examine the car too. There's no one in it, just a fur coat, a grey jacket, and thrown carelessly on to the dashboard, a tube of red lipstick. There's a leaflet for the zoo lying on the seat.

It's got a picture of the penguins on it. They look happy, but then the photograph doesn't show their tiny concrete pool.

"What do you think about the penguins?"

"In the zoo?"

"I mean — it's wrong, yes? Keeping them like that?"

"Yes — it's definitely not right. It's cruel, but there's nothing we can do about it. I mean, I suppose we could give our pocket money to the zoo and write to the World Wildlife Fund or something."

I suck on a mint humbug. Disgusting. "We could

do something bigger than that, something really positive. I'm sure there's a way to change things for the penguins."

Ellie pops a bubblegum in her mouth.

"S'pose so. What've you got in mind?"

I Bet David Attenborough's Never Done This

It's dark when I prod Ellie awake.

"Are you ready for this?" I ask.

"Totally," she says, in a way that doesn't convince me.

We slip down the stairs and into the kitchen. I've got Dad's tools in an old shoulder bag and I slip my feet into Mum's slightly big flowery wellies.

I'm taking both my parents on this trip but I still feel absolutely terrified.

We need Syd's pushchair for the job, but it's buried under a pile of junk in the hall. Ellie lifts up the badminton set, and a load of marbles skiddle across the floor.

We freeze.

There's a creak from Mum's room. I hold my breath as she comes out on to the landing and goes into the bathroom.

We hear her wash her hands, then without even looking down the stairs, she goes back to bed, shutting the bedroom door behind her.

I breathe again.

This time, Ellie pulls the pushchair while I take the blankets off the heap and lay them on the floor, so that anything that escapes will fall silently.

Outside, there's a sliver of moon lighting our way. I can see pretty well in the dark, but Ellie's hopeless and she has to watch the reflective strip on Mum's wellies to work out where she's going.

The footpath seems lumpier by moonlight, and longer, and Syd's rubbish pushchair weighs a ton.

By the time we reach the edge of town, there's a faint glimmer of light over the sea.

"Is that dawn?" asks Ellie.

"Suppose so."

"I've never seen dawn," she says. "That's quite exciting."

I'm amazed by the things that Ellie finds exciting.

The white walls of the zoo glow faintly, but otherwise everything's in a grainy black and white.

I walk up to the main gate.

"Why have you stopped?" hisses Ellie. "I'm scared, Scarlett. Suppose someone sees us."

"Don't worry, it'll be fine," I say, wishing I believed it.

To our left, there's an office building with alarms and shiny glass doors, but the door for the general public is just a big padlock and a gate.

I take Dad's tools out of my bag and start to fiddle with the padlock.

"What are you doing?" she hisses.

"Unlocking it, how else are we supposed to get in?"

I wriggle the long pick inside the lock, but nothing happens.

"What are you doing now?"

"Still trying to unlock it."

I try all the picks and the bump key and then a long, hooked thing that's in a different part of the pouch.

Ping.

"I've done it! We're in."

But we aren't, because although we're through the outer gate, I've forgotten about the turnstiles inside. They're set on letting people out, or letting people with pound coins in, and I haven't got a pound coin. I stare at them for a minute, there's no lock, no way to break in. You can't climb under them.

"Now what?" says Ellie, measuring herself against the turnstile. It stops just below her chin.

I put one hand on top and vault over. Ellie stands outside with the pushchair, looking confused.

"Jump over," I say.

"I can't, Scarlett, it's too high."

"You've got to, there's no other way – I can't unlock them."

There's this silence, and I can hear her cagoule rustling.

"Come on, Ellie, give it a go."

"Ah – there we are," she says. "I've found a pound in my pocket."

She slots the coin into the turnstile, and it swings round, allowing her through, holding the pushchair above her head.

"There," she says. "Now what?"

* * *

The zoo's creepy in the early morning. Things stamp up and down in their pens, growling, while other things chirrup and whoop. It's too dark to see in properly, so we can only guess at what's going on. We have to walk through this almost completely black tunnel to the rest of the zoo. It's lined with cages, and I can sense animals racing up and down the bars.

"Whooooooohoooooo," something howls to the left.

"Yikes," squeals Ellie.

Something else lets out a scream like a banshee.

"Monkey?" she asks, her voice shaking.

"Hoo hoo hoo," laughs something large and dark. I can feel the wind as it leaps along the bars of a big pen.

This time I jump.

We creep through the dark patch. I can't see anything; my eyeballs are practically popping out, I'm trying so hard. But I can certainly hear, and smell, and that smell is pretty rough – poo, wee and animal bad breath.

It's hot down here too, so when we break out of the dark into the main part of the zoo, the air seems cool and fragrant.

"Whoa," says Ellie.

"Whoa," I agree.

We wheel the pushchair round past the sleeping panda, and the flamingos, who are doing what flamingos do in the mornings, until we reach the butterfly house. It looks horribly dark.

"You go first," says Ellie.

So I push open the flaps and run past all the sleeping butterflies, the creeping frogs and the floppy tendrils that brush my face.

"Ugh," says Ellie behind me. "That went right round my neck."

But it's not far to the end of the butterfly house, and we break out into the fresh air, which is when I suddenly feel really sick.

The Great Escape

Penguins stink.

Few things can possibly smell as bad as a penguin – maybe a wheelie bin, or the boys' toilets at school – but I don't believe it. I think when we normally see them at a zoo or somewhere, someone's been round with a broom and a high-powered hose, because at five o'clock in the morning, they're toxic.

"Whew," says Ellie.

I nearly throw up last night's supper, but swallow, and step over the side of the penguin enclosure as if I was used to mucking out fish-eating birds on a daily basis.

The penguins stand in their little pool, staring at me.

"Here, little penguin," I say to the smallest. He steps towards me, and I notice that he's looking at my hand as if it's a fish.

We should have brought gloves.

"Here," says Ellie. "Try this." She takes the lid from a dustbin that's been left in the corner of their pen. A new smell, like a fishmonger's mixed with boys' toilets and drains, wafts into the still, morning air. Ellie hands me a pair of thick orange rubber gloves. Breathing only through my mouth, I reach in and take something that might once have been a sardine. I throw it on the ground.

The little penguin gobbles it up and the two bigger penguins move in for a closer look.

"Quick," says Ellie, grabbing the biggest one from behind. It squawks, poos and snaps at her. I hold its beak shut, while Ellie lifts it up, and between us, we carry it over to Syd's pushchair, and using all of Syd's straps, pin it until it stops struggling.

"One down, two to go."

"But how are we going to carry them?" she asks.

The little penguin fits my sweatshirt surprisingly

82

well, and Ellie's cagoule does a neat job of containing the other large one. I fill my bag with putrid bits of fish, take the pushchair and the small penguin while Ellie takes the other big one, and it's all fine until we reach the turnstiles.

It's not that we can't walk out through the turnstiles, they work perfectly well when you're trying to get out; it's just that they aren't big enough for a pushchair. Or a child and a penguin, or a child and a pushchair and a penguin.

It's one of those chicken, fox, slug, lettuce crossing the river things. I really don't know what to do first. The idea of letting a penguin loose on the streets of Dampmouth Bay makes my blood run cold.

Rats.

Perhaps we're mad, completely bonkers, if we think we can do this. Perhaps we should have gone to Amnesty International or the World Wildlife Fund or someone like that.

Then Ellie has an almost brilliant idea.

"Why don't they just walk through the turnstiles themselves – either one at a time, or all three at once?"

I gaze at the penguins. They've been very

accommodating so far; perhaps they'd like nothing better than a walk through a turnstile. "Maybe if you wave a sardine at them."

Ellie goes through first, and I slot the three penguins into the turnstile. They stop and look up at me hopefully.

"Go on," I say to them. "Freedom is that way." I point out of the zoo, through the turnstile, but the penguins just snap at my hand as if it was battered cod.

"Hand me some fish," says Ellie.

I reach into the bag and something slimy slips into my fingers.

"Ugh," I say.

"Ugh," says Ellie, when I hand it to her.

I fold up the pushchair and use it to block the back of the turnstile, so that the penguins can't suddenly decide they want to go back to their miserable pond.

"Here, pengy, pengy, here's some lovely stinky fish," says Ellie from the other side.

Like people watching tennis, all three penguins turn in her direction but they don't move.

"Come on, pretty pengies, come to Auntie Ellie."

They still don't move. It's perfectly true that

you can't expect a creature born to live in the wide cold Antarctic to understand that when you push against this particular iron bar it rolls forward and lets you through.

I nudge the turnstile and it knocks into the big penguin at the back. He shuffles forward into the smaller penguin, who stamps on the little penguin. They all move forward a nanometre.

"S'working," says Ellie. "Crikey," she says. "Look at that." She points to the sky. She's right, everything's turning from black and white to colour, like someone's turned on a switch. Morning won't be long.

The penguins shuffle through the turnstile and I jam myself in the slot behind them, clutching the folded pushchair that now whiffs of pilchard.

"Ow!" Ellie yowls. "More fish, Scarlett, quick."

"I can't move, not until the penguins move."

I push a little harder, and the turnstile gives way, throwing me out of the gate on to the pavement. The penguins surround Ellie; they're studying her, expecting more fish. Perhaps they even think she is a fish, a pale blue grubby fish with glasses.

She looks awesome, and I don't mean in a good way. Her clothes are coated with silver fish scales and blood, suggesting a mermaid that's been caught in a hideous seaside accident, and I can't believe she can see anything through her steamed-up glasses. The penguins look pretty special too: Ellie's cagoule fits the middle one quite well, although something's going on with the hood. The little one's managed to smear a fishy slick all down the front of my sweatshirt, much like Syd after breakfast. The big one's eyeing the builder's yard next door, wondering whether to eat Ellie first, or dive into a pile of sand.

They all decide to eat Ellie first.

"Do something!" she yelps.

I fumble in my bag. There's practically nothing left, just some slime and crunchy bits. Tails? I hold the bag upside down, and a few flakes land on the concrete. The penguins take their eyes off Ellie and scrabble to pick up the fish.

"Quick!" I yell. "Get them!" The big one gets right down on his belly and snuffles at the concrete, so we grab him and truss him in the pushchair.

I swoop on the baby, and Ellie pins the middle-sized one down.

The penguins don't seem to be a bit bothered.

Freedom

There's another thing I've discovered about penguins this morning, and that is that they're heavy.

It takes us about a year to get back to the watercress beds. I expect Syd's nearly awake by now,

"Come on, Ellie," I say, looking back. She's red in the face, but the penguin looks quite comfy.

The other thing with the penguins is that they're slippery, which makes them hard to hold on to; it looks like fur on the outside, but it isn't, it's feathers, because after all, they are birds.

We struggle up over the stile, and at last I can see

the big tank behind the watercress beds.

So, I think, can my penguins.

The little one's really wriggling now. "Stop it!" I say, tying the arms of the sweatshirt around him for the millionth time. "Stop it – I'm not doing this for fun, you know, it's for your own good."

He looks up at me and I could swear he smirks.

The last fifteen metres is grim. The pushchair gets stuck in every rut, my hair keeps falling over my eyes, my nose is itching, I'm hot and everything smells awful.

I break it down into paces. *One two three four, one two three four*. Past the airfield control tower.

One two three four, one...

Yay! The watercress beds at last.

I undo the straps on the pushchair and lift the big penguin out, avoiding his beak.

"Well, go on, then," says Ellie, taking the cagoule off the middle one, and untying the sweatshirt from the little one. "Have a swim."

I splash my hand in the water.

The penguins stand there watching me like I'm a telly.

"Perhaps they can't swim?" I say.

"All penguins can swim, like fish, of course they can." But I can tell from Ellie's voice that she's not so sure.

I reach into the bag. There are some scraps, so I empty it over the tank, and like synchronised swimmers, all three dive in.

It's amazing.

Fantastic.

Awesome.

"Whoa," says Ellie.

"Whoa, whoa," I say.

The penguins plunge around each other, like swallows diving. The water's deep here, but glass-clear, so I can see them at the bottom, darting down and swooping up. I can't tell, because penguins don't really do facial expressions, but I'm sure they're smiling.

The big one swoops up on to the concrete side of the tank, waddles out and dives back in, sliding past the other two to pop out on the far side.

"Yay!" squeals Ellie.

"We did it," I say.

"We made a difference," she says.

Bong, says the town hall clock. *Bong bong bong bong bong.*

"Argh," I say, and dragging the pushchair across the garden, we wave goodbye to the penguins and creep back inside.

Penguin vs
Watercress

Glowing with good deeds, we sneak up the stairs to my room. Everything is just as we left it and although there's light coming through the curtains, Syd seems to be asleep.

"What are we going to do with these?" Ellie pulls off her stinky pale blue jeans.

I have the brilliant idea of jamming them in a bin liner. I stick mine in there too and then stuff it under my bed. "We'll wait for Mum to go out and put them in the washing machine later."

Ellie goes to the bathroom and I wait by the window, watching the tank. There isn't much to see, but every now and again a black head bobs up.

I feel kind of warm and right. Here they are, the penguins, free and happy, able to swim deep in the tank and eat all the shrimps and crayfish that lurk at the bottom. We've been good – I've been good. I've used Dad's tools in the right way. Tools and a little determination.

"Yes," I say out loud. "Yes, I've done the right thing, Dad – I've done what you'd have done."

I'm practically popping with the feeling of good things.

"Yes," I say one more time.

The big penguin clambers out of the tank and stands on the side. He's not looking at the big tank this time, he's eyeing the watercress beds themselves; twelve green strips of fresh young watercress.

He waddles down the ramp from the tank towards the nearest bed and flops into the water. It's less than ten centimetres deep, but he turns and wallows, and scratches his back in the little plants, leaving a scar right across the bed.

"No, don't do that," I mutter.

He pushes off from the side and swings himself right across the bed, mowing a dark stain.

The penguin throws himself back on to the bank

and pads up towards the big tank again.

Phew, but I'm thinking about that dustbin full of fish. Do they eat one of those every day? Every week? Every hour?

Where are we going to find enough fish?

Ellie joins me at the window. "What's that big brown patch on the end watercress bed?" she asks.

"The big one got out of the tank and tried the beds, but he went back in, not too much damage, not really. They still look really happy," I say. "It's brilliant." Although my happy feeling has a touch of grey creeping in around the edges.

"Yes," says Ellie. "It's fantastic." But she sounds flat as she says it.

"Yeah," I say, still staring from the window.

"Scarlett?"

"Yes?"

"What happens if they won't stay in the tank?"

Penguin vs
Paddling Pool

"Aaaaaaaarhghghghghghghg!"

It's Mum, and her scream brings me wide awake. I must have fallen asleep on my bed because the sun's streaming in through the window and I can hear Syd yelping in the garden in an I've-been-awake-for-ages kind of a way.

"What?" Ellie leaps out of bed.

I stay where I am. I think I can guess exactly what's happened.

"Oh, Scarlett, look."

Ellie pulls back the curtains so that there's no way I can't see what's happened.

The twelve green watercress beds have now become twelve muddy pools surrounded by concrete. And there's no sign of the penguins.

"Whoa," I say. "Where have they gone?"

"There." Ellie points straight down.

The three penguins lie in what's left of Syd's paddling pool, wallowing in the mud, tearing chunks of plastic from the sides. One of them's got Mum's flowery wellies in his mouth.

"Whoops," says Ellie.

A string of much ruder words go through my head.

"Scarlett!?" Mum yells up the stairs.

"I'm dead," I say to Ellie, stepping out on to the landing.

"Scarlett – has this got anything to do with you?"

For a moment I consider lying, but then I realise that it's wrong to lie, and more importantly, that the fishy, slimy pushchair is still standing round the back of the house like a huge clue.

Rats.

"Um," I say, and Mum beckons me down. She's already got the phone in one hand and she's flicking through the directory with the other.

Syd's inside, his face pressed to the kitchen

window, watching the penguins.

" 'Engy, art-lett, 'engy," he says, looking about as excited as it's possible to look.

"Blast," says Mum. "They're not there yet."

"Who?"

"The zoo, no one's answering the phone. I'll have to ring Derek."

Rats.

"Derek?" says Mum. "There are three penguins in Syd's paddling pool, the zoo hasn't opened yet, and they're tearing the pool apart. We need help." She listens to the phone again. "I don't know how they got there." She stares at me, very hard. "No – but they seem to think this is home, they're quite big, and sort of savage, no, not like a tiger – please, come quick – oh, and, Derek, buy some fish on the way, yes, from anywhere, the corner shop'll do – no – I'm sure they'll manage the bones, they don't seem to have had any trouble eating the watering can."

Mum slams down the phone, turns to me and says, "Explain."

Cat vs Penguin

There's a fire engine parked in the middle of the watercress beds. It's between the Dampmouth Bay Radio van, and Uncle Derek's police car. Mr Hammond, the man who owns the watercress beds, is weeping into a microphone, while a cameraman films the devastation. Six zoo keepers stalk the little penguin with a large net, but he's happy leaping from the tank into the beds and back again.

They came with a bath load of fish; Uncle Derek came with six boil-in-the-bag kippers and a packet of fish fingers.

The firemen look overdressed for the weather,

but I suppose they're here because they've got big wellies, and yellow waterproofs that don't mind the smell of fish.

Ellie and I offered to catch the little penguin with the cagoule and a sardine, but everyone just glared at us.

I think we've learned a lot about penguin behaviour this morning, I bet none of that lot have coaxed a penguin through a turnstile. We're experts.

They let us visit the two larger ones, who are in a kind of pod, trailer thing.

"They're very hungry," says a woman who seems to be an official penguin feeder.

"Oh," I say, thinking about the sticklebacks and minnows they've had in the tank. "Do they eat a lot?"

"Each penguin eats about three kilos of fish per day, often more."

Ellie raises her eyebrows. "So how long would they have survived here?"

The woman shrugs. "A few hours? Your guess is as good as mine."

A few hours? That explains why they didn't stay in the big tank. But there can't have been much to eat in the watercress beds, not unless they'd become vegetarians overnight. They must have been starving.

Then there's a load of shouting, and the little penguin takes a passing snap at Syd's paddling pool and races into the house through the kitchen door.

"Yeouwwwwwww!" That's Houdini the cat. The penguin doesn't make any sound at all. Perhaps he's examining our kitchen, or maybe he's eaten Houdini. Cat vs Penguin. Would Houdini even recognise that the penguin's a bird?

The penguin doesn't come out, but then, nor does the cat.

The fish-feeding woman starts towards the back door, and so do six firemen, five zoo keepers and Uncle Derek. As they cram in through the door, Houdini slips through their legs like a small stegosaurus, the fur on his back standing up in spikes. Close behind, the penguin tries to do the same thing, but he's four times the size, slow and not as clever as the cat. He's grabbed by a fireman.

"Gotcha!" the man shouts before the penguin bites him hard on the hand. "Ow!" And for a second the penguin's free again, before a zoo keeper throws a net over his head and the great escape is stopped dead in its tracks.

More cars have arrived at the watercress beds: WCTV, the RSPCA and three unmarked vans with camera equipment. Uncle Derek's turned into a parking warden, and Mum's standing outside the house with an expression of apocalyptic rage on her face.

The TV people film us and Mum and the penguins.

The zoo people pack the last penguin into the trailer.

"Bye, 'engy," says Syd.

I can't actually speak. I was so sure we were doing the right thing, and it's all ended like this.

Mum Goes
Ballistic

The first thing we have to do is apologise to Mr Hammond.

"Sorry," I say. "I'm really sorry."

"Yes, so am I," says Ellie.

Mr Hammond looks devastated and Uncle Derek leads us back into the house.

He doesn't need to say anything to us.

We got the message.

Uncle Derek and Mum sit on one side of the table. Ellie and I sit on the other.

Syd's drawing on the back of the kitchen door

with Mum's lipstick, but Mum's obviously not going to tell him off, she's devoting every last scrap of fury to me.

Uncle Derek keeps clicking his stopwatch until Mum lays her hand over his.

"Sorry, Carole," he says, and he starts to tap his foot on the ground under the table instead.

Mum's pinched her lips so much that her mouth has almost disappeared. Her face is white with tiny pink circles on her cheeks. I'm not sure I've ever seen her this cross.

"Scarlett, Ellie," she says so quietly that we strain forward to listen. "WHAT IN HADES DID YOU THINK YOU WERE DOING!"

We all jump, even Uncle Derek. Syd puts down the lipstick and tries to wipe the drawing from the door with a pair of Mum's pants.

"Sorry, Auntie Carole," says Ellie. "But we thought we were doing the right thing—"

"RIGHT THING, RIGHT THING?" Mum's gone completely red now. "How could it possibly be the right thing with that circus going on out there? Penguins! Penguins, of all things? What on earth possessed you both?" She slams her hand on the table. Ellie jumps. "God only knows what you've done to the poor creatures…"

"And the TV cameras," says Uncle Derek, arranging the three hairs of his moustache in the mirror by the door. "They weren't good."

Mum stares at him. "Cameras? They're the least of our worries, what about the actual damage? No wonder those penguins live in a concrete compound, they're complete vandals. They've destroyed everything. We'll have to pay hundreds of pounds for the watercress beds, probably thousands, and don't firemen charge when you call them out these days? And there was the poor man that got bitten."

No one's mentioned the paddling pool or the watering can or Mum's wellies.

Uncle Derek gets up and walks round the table so that he's standing behind us. "I don't think the fire boys'll charge this time, not after what they did to your garden." When the fire engine left, it had to reverse over Mum's vegetable patch to get out. It drove off down the road with the runner bean poles sticking out of the hoses. Syd thought it was really funny. Mum didn't.

"And the zoo – will they prosecute?" She turns to Uncle Derek.

He shrugs. "Breaking and entering, strictly speaking. And you are old enough to take criminal responsibility. But I doubt it. I'll give them a ring in a bit."

I suddenly feel sick. I'd never thought that we'd broken the law.

There's a silence at the table that's as thick as porridge.

Ellie's in tears next to me. I don't suppose she's ever been told off like this.

Mum's off again. "Did it never occur to you that penguins are wild animals that need to eat a shed load of fish every day, and that they're in a zoo because a zoo has people who are trained to look after them? Eh?"

Ellie shakes her head. I do too. I really don't think I can speak any more.

"And have either of you idiots ever read the notice next to the penguin enclosure?"

We shake our heads again.

"Well, if you'd ever bothered, it would have told you that the zoo's trying to raise money to send them to a fabulous animal park in Canada, where they'll have vast amounts of space and as much salmon as they can eat. Money that it's now going to take longer to raise because they've wasted some of it on this morning's escapade."

Mum stands up and sits down again. She puts her glasses on and takes them off as if she's so cross she can't even remember why she was wearing them.

"So why? Why did you do it?" Mum's all staring and mad now. I really don't want to say anything.

"Because the penguins were in a tiny pen, without any water?" Ellie offers.

"Because it was cruel to keep them there?" I chip in as quietly as I can.

Mum gazes at us as if we're the most stupid people she's ever seen. "Go on."

"We were trying to do what Dad did," I say.

"Yeah," says Ellie. "We just thought we could put things right. Like Scarlett's dad did."

Mum looks puzzled.

I hear Uncle Derek let out a long sigh behind us. "Did you use your dad's tools to get into the zoo?"

I nod.

"What?" says Mum, staring from Uncle Derek to me and back again. "Tools?"

Uncle Derek takes a huge breath in. "Scarlett," he says. "Have you told your mum about the tools?"

I shake my head, reach into my backpack, which is under the table, and pull out the tools.

Mum gasps. "Where did they come from?"

Pigs Might Fly

It doesn't go down well, the whole tools business, and I can see that Ellie's dying to blurt out that there were other things in the box too, but somehow, she stays silent.

Mum confiscates the tools and then can't work out whether she's more furious with me or Uncle Derek, or even Dad. She sends us to bed ridiculously early, which is just as well because I feel such an idiot that hiding under my duvet is the only thing I can face. We don't even talk to each other. Instead we lie in silence, listening to the summer sounds outside and to Mum and Uncle Derek having their first row.

I think it's supposed to be a secret row, but they're in the garden and the window's open and they're rubbish at whispering.

"I still can't believe you told her about her father. You idiot!"

"She's got a perfect right to know." Uncle Derek's jogging, I can hear his feet. "In fact, I thought she already knew. I'm sorry, but she gave me that impression. Anyway, it's awful living all your life thinking your dad's a criminal."

Mum's digging, I can hear the spade hitting the earth too hard. "But she was fine, just fine before that. If you hadn't told her she'd never have had such a silly idea."

"Well, I'm sure you know her best, she's your daughter, but she wasn't all right." Uncle Derek clicks his stopwatch. "She'd got the tools, and wanted to use them." He stops clicking his stopwatch. "At least she just did something stupid. In fact, Carole, they were only trying to do something good — it was just horribly misjudged."

"Misjudged?" squeals Mum. "It was mad! I didn't think she could do anything so stupid."

"I didn't think Ellie could either, but they might

have done something much worse with those tools ... something criminal."

I flush under my bedclothes.

"What was Dick thinking of?" says Mum. "Giving them to her? I mean, honestly."

Uncle Derek speaks, but one of them drags a bucket over the gravel so I can't hear his answer. I strain to hear any more conversation.

"Well, it was up to me to tell her about her dad," says Mum. "Not you."

"I couldn't agree more," says Uncle Derek.

For a while all I hear is the trickle of the stream into the watercress beds and the sound of Mum's spade.

"But you didn't tell her all that nonsense about the diamonds?"

"I did," says Uncle Derek.

"What?" Something loud and heavy hits the ground. "Why?"

"Every little girl's got to believe in something, haven't they? She's a bit old for fairies – anyway, it might all be true."

"Pigs might fly," mutters Mum.

"Fair enough, but it's only what the rest of the world thinks."

"Maybe you're right. I'm just worried about her."

Uncle Derek must have walked over to Mum, because the next bit's muffled. "I'll keep an eye," he says. "A closer eye."

I lie there waiting for more, but they've gone quiet now. Instead I listen to Syd singing to his teddy.

What's Black and White
and Red All Over?

"What did the penguin cop shout at the snowman robber?" shouts Sam Lewis. "Freeze!"

"What's black and white and red all over?" asks Melissa.

"A sunburned penguin!" shouts Jessica.

"Why did two penguins jump when they first met?" asks Sam Lewis.

"Don't know," says Amber.

"They were trying to break the ice," says Sam. "Get it?"

Ellie and I walk quickly into class. Mrs Gayton's sitting with a smug smile on her potato face.

"Cops and robbers," she says. "Fancy."

I go over and sharpen some pencils.

Ellie shuffles in her book bag.

"Well, it's just what I've come to expect of a child like you, Scarlett McNally. Thoughtless behaviour that's caused Lord knows how much trouble." Mrs Gayton leans back on her chair. "When I was in the paratroopers, we had an insolent little private like you. Came to a sticky end. Breaking rocks at Her Majesty's Pleasure, these days."

I stare hard at the pencils.

I could throttle her.

Ellie and I separate on the way home. She lives in a very clean white house on an estate of clean white houses. Inside, everything has somewhere to live. Uncle Derek never buys a box of cereal that won't fit in the cupboard, or a milk container that won't fit in the door of the fridge. Ellie's never missed a single lunch payment, or brought the wrong pair of socks for PE.

At home we get everything wrong and I'm always late with things, but Uncle Derek is scarily organised.

He's looked after Ellie since her mum walked out

on them, although I don't know when that was, and he's been helping Mum out since she sent Syd's dad to South America. Now I'm wondering how much that's because he's been paid to hang around, and how much it's because he wants to.

It's been about a year now.

I suppose Uncle Derek's all right really, it's just he's such an alien. All that soap powder and fabric conditioner and things that smell of supermarkets.

Ellie loves him to bits, even though he's a dad, not a mum. I guess she's making the best of it; after all, you can live perfectly well without a dad.

Mums are much more important.

I can't imagine life without Mum.

I don't go straight home; instead, I pass the back of the zoo. There are these tall concrete walls all around it. I could probably climb over them, but I've got some coins and after four o'clock, you can get through the turnstiles for fifty pence.

Anyway, I think I've done enough in the way of breaking in. I don't want to draw any attention to myself; although I don't suppose the zoo keepers would recognise me in my school uniform.

Outside the front is the long black car again. I stop to look at the little flag, sticking out of the end of the bonnet. It's got the three royal starfish of Dampmouth Bay Council, the same as all the wheelie bins, so it's definitely the mayoress's car.

Weird. Funny how you never see something then you come across it twice in one week.

Inside, I ignore the grubby undersized panda, and the stinky stick-insect house. I pass the flamingos and the screaming monkeys and head straight for the back.

The penguins are there. The three of them. One standing, two lying in their little pond. It's honestly no bigger than Syd's paddling pool. There's a big notice in front of them and this time I read it. Mum was right, they are trying to send them to some grand zoo in Canada.

Ellie and I should have looked.

We were so stupid. We'll never live it down.

I lean on the railings round the enclosure and stare, and feel sad for them. I feel sad for me and Ellie too, although I'd swear the little one smiles at me, which makes me feel less sad.

"Awful, innit," says a man's voice next to me.

"Mm," I say, watching the smallest penguin try to swim.

"Like theft," he says.

"Ah," I say.

"Theft, you see, is always wrong."

I slide my eyes as far to the right as they'll go. All I can see is a grey sleeve. I take a step to my left, towards a family at the other end.

"Yes, big theft, little theft," he says. "It's all the same to me."

I take another step to my left, but there's this fur coat in my way, and a set of scary red fingernails holding on to it. I follow the fingernails to the hand, and the hand to the arm. But I already know what I'm going to find at the top.

"S'funny really, how thieving runs in families," says the man in the grey suit. "Used to know this bloke, clever fella, always sneakin' about. In and out of windows, palaces, offices, high-security places. Took a lot of stuff, he did. 'E was a thief."

I step back from the rail. My heartbeat's gone mad, and I can hardly breathe. He's wearing the chauffeur's cap, as if he's on official duty. He steps back with me, following me over to the butterfly house. He touches my arm and I look up into his face.

He's got a yellowed grey moustache, coffee-stained teeth and his breath smells of fish and chips.

"It's just that bloke I was telling you about, he got paid in diamonds. I'd love to know what he did with them. I've been wondering for years, but a little bird told me that his younger relation has recently received a gift, and blow me down if I didn't see that younger relation on the telly the other day, surrounded by penguins."

He's got piggy little bloodshot eyes. Tired eyes.

"Oh," I say, pulling away and walking quickly towards the gift shop.

"A present, I believe, for her eleventh birthday." He falls into step beside me. "One that might contain a message? Perhaps?"

"I don't know what you're talking about," I say breathlessly.

"I believe that that younger relation, his daughter, perhaps, might now know the location of those diamonds."

The woman closes in on my other side.

"I've been waiting, see?" she says. "I've been waiting for years, and now I want my diamonds."

"Have you?" The gift shop's only five or six metres away. "And why would his daughter give you the present from her father? Why wouldn't she tell the police?"

The man tugs on my arm, and although I don't want to, I have to turn and face him. "I've reason to believe his daughter might have taken one or two things in her time. Things she shouldn't 'ave." He pats his pocket. "I've a little CCTV footage from the mayoral office, shows a narky little sneak thief half-inching a load of sweeties."

CCTV?

Of course, Uncle Derek said it, the whole town's covered by CCTV from the council offices.

Stupid, stupid, me. But I manage to say: "Oh?" really casually.

"Yes – and I believe I could help her avoid the long arm of the law, if she'd only give me a certain box." He catches my sleeve again, but only gently. "It's just a question of right and wrong, you see, Scarlett, just a question of right and wrong."

I Wish I Was
Someone Else

I run all the way home. And when I get there, I lock all the windows, even the tiny one in the bathroom that only Syd can get through.

When Mum comes home from work with Syd, I try really hard to tell her about the lady mayoress and her chauffeur, but I can't. If she knew I'd broken into the sweet shop on top of yesterday's penguin fiasco, she'd put me up for adoption, and anyway she'd never believe that the lady mayoress would do anything wrong.

So I watch baby TV with Syd and let him draw on my face. I wouldn't normally let him draw on my face, I'd rather let a slug crawl over me, but I need to do "good" things.

I build Syd a long and complicated train track. He destroys it, and I build him another one. He destroys that, and I build him another one. I even push a train around it.

"Are you all right, Scarlett?" Mum asks.

I nod, and redesign the station, and worry.

We eat yellow eggs and home-grown broad beans, and Mum makes plum crumble for pudding.

I hate broad beans, but I eat them anyway.

After supper, I give Syd his bath. He gives me a foam moustache and beard.

I even help him into his pyjamas.

At bedtime, Mum asks, "Are you sure you're OK?"

And I wait a really long time before saying, "Fine, Mum, just tired."

Mum feels my forehead, tucks us both into bed, and sings songs to us until I'm on the edge of sleep.

I wish I was someone else.

I'm going to get Mum to drive me to school tomorrow.

Today Is
Mostly Ropes

Although I dream of large women in leopard-skin coats, never once has it crossed my mind that I should give up the box. Well, not till now. It's assembly, and Mrs Mason, the head teacher, is whining on about semi-colons so everyone's doodling and passing notes. I'm replaying the conversation at the zoo.

If she'd only give me a certain box.

So I could just do it. I could give the chauffeur the box, and that would be that, problem solved.

Phew.

And then I think about Dad, about the little

collection of things he bothered to send me. The little clues about his life, the pictures, even the tools. They only want the box because of the diamonds, and the diamonds don't exist, and they shouldn't have it anyway, because it's mine. He gave it to me.

But then they're going to tell Mum about the sweets.

I hate this.

I look across at Ellie; she's the only person paying any attention to Mrs Mason. She's also the only person I can talk to about this.

Funny that, I wouldn't have thought it a week ago.

The lesson bell rings.

I follow Ellie down the corridor to the PE shed, but I can't get close, there's a cluster of boys dancing sideways, and I can't reach her.

"Ellie," I call, but she's gone through the changing-room doors. I bash through them with my shoulder and stop dead.

Mrs Gayton's standing in the middle of the changing room, already changed. Mrs Gayton used to be in the army, and you can really see it now. Although she's ancient she's wearing a sleeveless vest and baggy military shorts. The most disturbing thing about it is the tattoo of a mermaid on her chicken-skin thigh. It's stretched and wrinkled and slightly green.

It's not something that innocent children should see.

Ugh.

She's prowling, looking like she wants to give us all very short haircuts or at the very least make us scrub floors and eat beetroot for the rest of our lives.

It's going to be gym today, I can tell, because Mrs Gayton's got bare feet. Bare, bunioned, calloused, veiny feet. Not that she actually does any gym herself. She just sneers at us and blows her whistles.

I think that if you peeled her skin back, she'd be green underneath. Like an alien.

But despite Mrs Gayton, I still feel pleased that it's gym, not rounders or tennis, because I'm rubbish at things with balls, and I'm brilliant at climbing and jumping things.

Today is mostly ropes.

I climb mine easily and swing a somersault over the bar at the top.

Luckily Mrs Gayton's got her back to me. She's focusing on Ellie.

"Come on, Ellie," she says. "Would you *please* try to climb the rope. Everyone." She gathers the class around. "Shall we watch Ellie try to climb the rope?"

The boys stop screaming and running about. The girls drop their skipping ropes and come to stare.

Ellie can't climb the rope. She can't even get above the knot at the bottom. She struggles and fights with it, until her arms and feet are pink.

"I'm sorry, Mrs Gayton," says Ellie. "I can't do it." She slips down to the floor.

"Exactly. Thank you, Ellie, you've just demonstrated, perfectly, how not to climb a rope."

Ellie's face flushes red to match her hands and the class laughs.

Rabbit Can Fly

I meet Ellie in the playground at lunchtime. She's been crying and she's holding her black rabbit, the one her mum gave her before she left.

"Where do you want to go?" I ask.

"Anywhere but here," says Ellie.

We sit in the willow, where the boys play. The boys are noisy, but they're not horrible. I feel safe in here, but I don't know about Ellie.

"Ellie," I begin. "You know the stuff from the sweet shop?"

"Yes?" she says, sucking her thumb and stroking the rabbit at the same time.

But we don't get to finish, because the Coven come over.

Melissa stands with her hands on her hips. Jessica's behind her, eating a chocolate bar.

"Would you like to show us how to climb the climbing frame, Ellie?" says Melissa in a sugary voice.

"I could hold your glasses," says Jessica. "They've got so much glass in them they might break."

"No thanks." Ellie pulls the rabbit tighter.

"Would *you* like to show us?" Melissa looks at me. "You could show us how your dad escaped from prison. Or how you stole the penguins?"

I ignore her.

"It's just we'd really like to know – how not to do it." Melissa turns to Jessica and they giggle together.

Ellie stares at the ground. I stare at Melissa's shoes. They've got puppies all over them. Soft cute puppies, but Melissa's not soft and cute. She's a witch.

I'm gazing at the shoes, imagining Melissa burning on the stake, when I see Ellie's rabbit fly across the playground.

"Wha—?" shouts Ellie, springing to her feet in shock.

I'm faster, but not quick enough to save the rabbit from a well-aimed lob on to the school roof.

Roof with
a View

It takes me about five minutes to get up there. There's one of those huge wheelie bins round the back of the school, and that, plus a drainpipe, is all I need. My arms really ache from the rope-climbing but I want Ellie to have her rabbit back.

I want to do the right thing for once.

And I want Melissa and Jessica to pay for always doing the wrong thing.

From the roof of the school the view's fantastic. It's a perfectly safe roof, flat, and covered in tarmac stuff. There's loads of rubbish up here: shoes, hats, lunch boxes, sandwiches, pencils, all wet and skanky, and the rabbit.

I wave at everyone in the playground. Ellie waves back, but Mrs Mason's face has gone a weird purple colour and Mrs Gayton's on the mobile phone, running towards me, talking really fast.

The Coven look genuinely shocked.

That'll show them.

I can't really hear anyone down there, because from up here, the bypass is noisier. And I can see it. Huge lorries thunder through the fields, and behind me, the sea glitters like a sheet of tinfoil. I can see everything, even the watercress beds.

It's magic. I should climb up here more often. I pick up some of the old rubbish, using a pencil for the soggy things, and drop them off the side. There's a squawk and I look over the edge to see Mrs Gayton, glaring up at me through the mossy glove that's just fallen on her glasses.

I pick up Ellie's rabbit and wave it in the air. Ellie waves back.

In the middle of town, a blue siren starts up, and I follow it through the streets all the way here. I feel like a homing device.

I stand and watch as a police car screams into the school yard and two men in uniform jump out.

One of them trips over the steps on the way up, the other's moving really fast. He's sprinting towards the school.

Uncle Derek.

But!

Uncle Derek sticks his head over the side of the roof and tells me to come down.

I think about saying nothing.

He's not my dad. He can't tell me what to do.

"Scarlett." His face is all serious.

"So?"

But he's actually looking me in the eye. And he actually looks quite worried.

"Scarlett, if you stay up there, I'll be forced to tell your mum," he says.

So I come down, and he helps me, and he doesn't get cross, just pats me on the back, and I follow

Mrs Gayton and Mrs Mason into Mrs Mason's office.

I've still got Ellie's rabbit stuffed down my trousers.

I should have given it to Uncle Derek.

Rats.

"But they took Ellie's rabbit, and they threw it on the roof!" I shout for the millionth time.

Mrs Mason sighs, leans back and stares at something she obviously finds really interesting on her desk. "That's not the point, Scarlett. The point is that you can't possibly go clambering around on the roof. Yes, I concede that it was wrong to throw the rabbit there in the first place, and I will have a word with Jessica and Melissa, but you just can't go around taking the law into your own hands." She slaps her hands on her desk as if to make her point. "I'd have thought you would already have learned that with the penguin episode."

Mrs Gayton's perched on the windowsill, nodding her head to every word. She's still wearing her PE kit.

"It's simply not your job," says Mrs Mason, smiling at me.

"But what about Ellie's rabbit — she can't sleep without it — who would have climbed up to get it?" I stare at Mrs Gayton.

"Me? Oh no," she squawks.

I imagine her climbing the ladder, giving us all a view up her army shorts.

Ugh.

"The caretaker would have gone to get it," says Mrs Mason.

"Oh yeah — in about another month? All that stuff I found up there's been there forever."

"Oh, Scarlett." Mrs Mason flaps her hand at me and looks really tired.

"But what would happen to Ellie? She can't manage without it. She wouldn't sleep at all. She hasn't got a mum."

"Calm down, Scarlett. Go back and finish your lunch, and I'll have a word with the other girls." She stands. "Go on, off you go."

"Aren't you going to punish her?" is the last thing I hear from Mrs Gayton, as the door closes behind me.

I head towards the door into the playground and I've just about made it outside when I feel a hand on my shoulder.

"Rabbit. Give it here." It's Mrs Gayton.

"What?"

She sticks out her bony hand. "Here, rabbit, now."

"No."

"Yes," she says, licking her lips.

"I won't, Mrs Mason didn't say I had to."

"Well, I say you do."

"What if I don't?"

But Mrs Gayton's faster than she looks and she grabs the rabbit right out of my trouser belt.

"Hey!" I yelp.

"Serve you both right," she snaps. "You and your ... your friend. I'm confiscating it."

"You can't!"

"I can, and did. Come and see me tomorrow to have it returned. Now go back to your lunch."

Promises,
Promises

When I get home, so angry I can hardly speak,
Mum's sitting outside with Syd. She's filling pots
with compost and sticking green things in them;
Syd's emptying them into his paddling pool and
making mud.

I throw down my school bag and stomp into the
house. I'm imagining Mrs Gayton in Antarctica
without a map.

Or a compass.

Or thick socks.

Or a woolly hat.

Or her favourite teddy.

"What's the matter, Scarlett?" Mum's leaning in the doorway.

"Everything. Nothing."

"Oh?"

So I tell her about Mrs Gayton and the rabbit. I don't tell her it was on the roof and that Uncle Derek came to get me down.

Mum comes to sit next to me. "I agree that it does sound wrong – she was never very nice, even when I was at school – but I suspect that you're not telling me the whole story."

"Uncle Derek told you?"

Mum shakes her head. "Not really. Mrs Mason rang."

"Oh," I say. "But did Uncle Derek tell you too?"

"Almost, not exactly."

So he did tell her.

Rats. Dad was right, I shouldn't trust just anyone.

I imagine Uncle Derek in the Antarctic.

Without his policeman's uniform.

Or his stopwatch.

Without Ellie.

"But it was still wrong," I say. "Poor Ellie – she's devastated."

"It was wrong of someone to throw the rabbit

on the roof, and it was probably wrong of Mrs Gayton to confiscate it, but it wasn't necessarily right for you to climb up and get it. It was almost right, but not completely right."

"But, Mum." I'm starting to feel really cross. "Things are either right or wrong."

"There are grey areas."

"Oh yeah – I've heard about grey areas from Ellie – does not telling me that Dad was a spy come into 'grey areas'?"

Mum goes pink. "What do you mean?"

"I mean that Uncle Derek – not you – told me about Dad. That Dad was really working as a sort of spy, and not a criminal after all." Mum tries to interrupt me but I'm not going to let her. "I've grown up all these years thinking he was a thief, and you let me... And you let THEM, beastly Mrs Gayton and the Coven and all of them, you let them think Dad was a thief and they've been attacking me with it ever since. You should have told me, then I could have ignored them. That would have been the right thing to do."

Mum looks like she's about to cry. "I'm sorry, I was just..."

"Uncle Derek has told me more about my dad

than you've ever done."

"Oh, Scarlett, that's not fair."

"None of this is fair." I sit back on the sofa.

"I was just..."

I stare at her. "Doing what you were told?"

Mum sinks on to the sofa next to me and curls her finger in my hair, but I pull away. "Mum, not now." I'm too angry.

She stands up and walks to the window. "I was probably scared of breaking the rules, yes, that and all the rumours about the diamonds. When you were little, how could I stop you going to school and blurting it out? Then we'd have been in trouble. I know you might think that's really silly and unimportant, but it wasn't; after your dad died there was so much speculation. People wanted to know where the diamonds were, and I didn't know, because I don't think they ever existed. All kinds of rumours went round about the way he died, and some of them were horrible." She traces her finger across the glass.

"I didn't want you to hear any of it, I wanted us to stay away — I wanted all of them to leave us alone. To hide here, away from it all. But there were inquests and endless police enquiries, and the men from MI5 and MI6 who couldn't stop asking questions. And I just had to stay silent and hope it would all die down, which, until now, it did."

"What about Uncle Derek?"

"What about him?"

"Is he a coincidence? Or…"

"He came because he was sent, love. But since then, things have changed."

"How?"

"He could go, if he wanted to, there's no danger any more."

I chew my lip. "Would you want him to?"

Mum sniffs and rearranges a cushion. "Scarlett, I'm sorry, you know – I'm really sorry I lied to you, told you that your dad was in prison, let you think he was a criminal." She looks up, meets my eye. "But you have to understand that I had to. I'd have loved to have told you the truth – I'd much rather you were proud of your dad. Of course I would, he was a wonderful human being…"

She sniffs again and, facing away from me, punches the cushion.

"But I needed to keep you safe."

Would You
Rather...

We've gone to bed. Ellie and me. But she's got no
rabbit and I can hear her crying under the covers.
She's sleeping over again because Mum's on early
morning duty at the care home.

Ellie wouldn't tell her dad about Mrs Gayton
stealing the rabbit, so I got Mum to promise not to
either, although she said she'd like to throttle Mrs
Gayton and would have a word with Mrs Mason.

This is my chance to tell Ellie about the lady
mayoress and her suited driver, but I don't think
she's in the mood to listen. It's funny, but I want
to talk to her now, I want her to know everything I

know, because although she dresses like a My Little Pony, and knows everything, and puts smiley faces over her "i"s, I like her being around. It's almost as if she's family.

I trust her. She's lied for me and I know she won't split.

"Ellie?"

"Yes."

"Do you want me to break into the school and get your rabbit back?"

"No."

"I could, you know. It'd be easy."

"No. You'll get into worse trouble. Thanks, but no. Anyway, your mum's got the tools, so you can't."

Shame. I know where the tools are now: under Mum's bed. I could break into the school anyway and write things about Mrs Gayton all over the gym wall.

Mrs Gayton smells.

Mrs Gayton smells worse than the boys' toilets.

Mrs Gayton is really an alien.

I could write it in green alien blood.

Then I have a picture of the two from the lady mayoress's car, watching me write on the wall.

And I shiver.

Anyway, I am supposed to be being good; I am supposed to be doing the right thing.

"Ellie?"

"Yes." There's a rustling and a cloud of washing-powder pong floats up into the room, although I don't mind it so much now. I've almost grown to like it.

"Would you rather..."

"What?" she says.

"Would you rather go on holiday with Mrs Gayton for a week or go for a run every day?"

"Go for a run."

"OK – would you rather go on holiday with Mrs Gayton, or sing 'Over the Rainbow' naked on stage, to the whole school?"

"Sing 'Over the Rainbow'. I'd even dance as well."

"OK." I think. "Would you rather go on holiday with her, or eat a slug?"

"Eat a slug."

"Two slugs?"

"I'd rather eat three slugs."

"A whole jug of slugs?"

"Yeurgh, a slug jug!" Ellie laughs.

"Ellie," I say, jumping up and banging my head on the top bunk. "The mayoress's driver, the man we saw in the butterfly house, tried to blackmail me the day after the penguins. He's got CCTV footage of me at the sweet shop."

Ellie's eyes are even bigger without glasses.

"Who?"

"The driver talked about clues, I don't know who he is." I remember the lady mayoress too, she wasn't exactly comforting. "And her, she talked about 'her diamonds' as if my dad took things from her."

"Dad said there was something odd about them."

"There is, they're creepy, and they keep appearing – or their car does."

"What do they want?" asks Ellie, her eyes glistening in the dark.

"The box. They want Dad's box."

What Are We Looking For?

We sit on the floor with my bedside light about a nanocentimetre from the rug so that the light doesn't show from outside.

We do not need a visit from Mum, or Uncle Derek.

Ellie spreads out the postcards, separating the photos and stacking them on one side.

"What are we looking for?" she asks.

"I don't know." I lay out the rest of the things from the box. "Anything we haven't seen before."

Gone with the Wind, turned down at page thirty-nine.

Key.

Message in a roll.

I could get the picklocks back from Mum's room, and put them in my school bag. We're not allowed sharp things at school, but if Mrs Gayton tries to take them away from me I'll play the Dead Dad card.

I don't know what I'll do if she pins me to the wall in a commando death grip. Give them to her, I suppose.

I flick through the photos, and a yellowed card pocket, about the size of a credit card, pokes out of the side. *Dampmouth Bay Library, Reference borrower's card.*

I hand it to Ellie. She squints under her glasses. "It's got Richard McNally written in pencil. Look."

I grab it off her – I can see what she means. Really faded pencil, in neat joined-up handwriting. Dad's?

I sniff it. It smells of old men's offices. How disappointing.

I peer inside; jammed at the bottom is a folded piece of pink paper.

My fingers won't fit, so I jab at it with a pencil, until Ellie takes off her glasses and we use the hooky piece that goes over her ear to drag it out.

It was obviously once the same size and shape as the card pocket. I flatten it against the rug.

On request. Letter Boxes, Dead and Live, *by G. G. Krimpas.*

"On request?" I say, staring at Ellie.

She stares back. "Library," she says firmly.

And I say, "Before school."

A Brief History
of Fish Paste

Uncle Derek's quiet this morning. He keeps looking at me, as if I might go off in some way. Presumably he's keeping an eye, like he said he would. He's not dressed, just wearing a pair of manly blue pyjamas that smell of fabric softener, and make the kitchen stink. I wonder if he washes his moustache with fabric softener to make it less scratchy.

He makes us perfect packed lunches, with neat pieces of ham, white bread and things in packets. Mum always gives me leftovers from the night before, sometimes delicious, but mostly embarrassing. It is not cool to bring a box of lentils and brown rice to school, no matter how yummy.

Not that I'm bothered.

"We're going early, Dad," says Ellie, shovelling in a last spoonful of cereal.

"I'll walk with you," says Mum. "Take Syd to nursery in the pushchair."

Ellie looks at me. "We're going to the library," I say.

"To look something up for homework," she adds quickly.

"That's fine," says Mum. "I'll come too."

We walk along by the airfield. Mum chats to Ellie and I walk ahead. I wish they'd hurry up, but I don't quite know how we're going to shake Mum off at the library. She's bound to ask questions.

We come out of the airfield on to the lane that leads across to the centre of town.

We walk for about two minutes before a car pulls up alongside us.

"Fancy a lift?" It's the lady mayoress's car. The driver's hanging out of the window in a cheery-chappy sort of way. "Going into town?"

"No," I say.

"Oh yes, town centre?" says Mum. "That would

be lovely, so kind. In you get, girls."

Ellie's frozen; so am I.

"Come on," says Mum, shoving Syd and his pushchair in through the rear door. "This is very kind of you."

"No problem, dearie," says the huge woman, making *coo-chee-coo* faces at Syd. "All public money, might as well use it for the public to enjoy — anyway, we all know about these two."

"Oh — yes, the penguins," says Mum, turning red. "Come on in, girls."

So we climb in.

"That was quite a thing, with those birds in your garden," says the lady mayoress.

"Wasn't it," says Mum. "Did you see it on the telly?"

" 'Engy…" says Syd, wiping his hands on the lady mayoress's skirt.

She gives him a sharp look before her face slides back into a smile. "We did, oh yes, we did — we saw you all on the telly, didn't we, Gerald?"

The driver grunts.

"We went to visit the penguins too, after — seeing as they'd become celebrities. Still, no harm done, eh?"

The car rolls silently through the lanes.

I'm jammed in between the lady mayoress and Mum. I can hardly breathe. Ellie's on a funny little seat that comes out of the back of the driver's. The driver should be sealed up in a glass cabin at the front, but the window's open so that he can hear us. It's like a proper black taxi inside, but much bigger. In fact, it's so big, you could put the whole of Golden Class in there.

And Mrs Gayton, and Mrs Mason.

"When did you move here?" asks Mum. "About three years ago?"

"Yes, I suppose it was," says the lady mayoress, fiddling with her handbag. She smells of make-up and thick perfume and theatres. She doesn't sound like a mayoress, she sounds more like the woman who runs the ghost train on the pier.

"How do you like it in Dampington?" asks Mum.

"Oh — well, it's been very pleasant, hasn't it, Gerald?"

The driver grunts in agreement.

"But you're from ... London?"

"Oh, yes." The lady mayoress looks uncomfortable. "We are — originally, but we like to think of ourselves as locals — don't we, Gerald?"

The driver grunts again.

"Where exactly are you going, dears?"

"Oh," says Mum. "The girls are off to the library to do some homework; I'm taking Syd to nursery."

"What a coincidence! We've got an appointment at the library this morning, haven't we, Gerald?" The lady mayoress calls through the car to the driver.

"Yes, dear, how convenient, we could take the girls all the way there."

Dear? Is that how the chauffeur addresses the lady mayoress? I wonder how she ever got elected. I look up at her, towering over me. She probably smothered the other candidates.

"That would be lovely," says Mum.

"No it wouldn't," I say, really quietly.

Mum pokes me. "Scarlett!"

I stare at the floor. This is really, really, *really* bad.

Mum strokes the sides of the car. "Lovely car, this."

"Oh yes, isn't it — look!" The lady mayoress presses a button and a door slides open. There's a little cupboard full of lit-up bottles and sparkly glasses.

"Oh," laughs Mum. "Wonderful."

Syd claps his hands. " 'Gain, 'gain."

"Isn't it lovely — means I can sneak a snifter between engagements." The huge woman laughs and her body laughs with her. I shake too; I've no choice, I'm so caught up in her pillowy sides.

She opens her handbag and pulls out a tube of sweets. "Like one?" she says, thrusting it under my nose. I refuse, but Syd takes three and crams them all in his mouth at once.

The car glides through the edge of town and pulls up silently by the library steps.

The driver springs round to open the door and we all pile out, Mum first, the lady mayoress last. Though she practically needs a hoist she's so big.

"Thank you so much." Mum beams and Syd waves as they push off down the road towards the nursery.

"Mum…" I call.

Mum turns round and blows a kiss. "See you later, Scarlett."

"Come on, girls," says the huge woman. "Up the steps."

Inside the library, I can hardly breathe. I'm clutching the little yellow pocket, and wondering quite how we can find anything out. The lady mayoress has gone to talk to the librarian.

The driver, on the other hand, is with us.

"Looking for books, are we?" he says.

"Yes." Ellie goes over to the reference section and crouches down by the bookstand in the middle of the room. I join her, pulling random books out and flicking through them, trying to look interested.

The driver goes behind the shelf and leans on it, his head hanging down over us.

"So, Scarlett – had a little think?"

I stay silent.

"Only we're getting a little impatient on our side of the deal, so I thought I'd up my offer, so to speak."

I rearrange the books in front of me. *Ghengis Khan, a Biography; A Brief History of Fish Paste.* Ellie's actually searching the shelves, but the man's not looking at her, he's staring at the top of my head, I can feel it.

"Now we've met your lovely mum, and your cute little brother, I thought perhaps we could get to know them better." He takes off his cap and twiddles it around on his forefinger. He's got almost no hair. For a second I think about landing a really heavy book on it. *50 Ways to Make Compost*, perhaps?

Ellie makes a small squeak. I don't look at her. I daren't.

"Anyway," the man goes on. "They're very nice, your family, and they fit in our car very nicely. They seem to trust us." He stands up and walks towards the main desk. "Shame if anything should happen to them."

Dodgems

We run all the way to school. Running's good because it makes me breathe, and I don't think I've done that for at least half an hour.

We haven't spoken either.

I don't want to discuss what the man said. I don't want it to be real. I want it to go away.

"I've got it," yells Ellie, panting behind me.

"What?"

"*Letter Boxes, Dead and Live.* I slipped it into my bag."

I stop, diving into a bus shelter.

"How?"

"It was there, in the shelves." She's so out of breath she can hardly speak.

"What! Let's see it."

Ellie takes it out. It's a small brown hardback, speckled with mildew. "Here," she says.

I hold the book in my hands and flick through the pages.

Nothing falls out, nothing's written inside, and there's nothing to say it's our copy.

Clangalangalangaclang.

School time.

I feel completely sick now. Completely like giving them the box, the key, all of it. Through maths I was thinking about Mum and Syd, they could be anywhere in the town, and no one would ever suspect the lady mayoress. Mum would just climb into that car and go…

Ellie doesn't seem to be worried. Maybe it's because her dad's a policeman, he can always rescue her — keep her safe. We're hiding out in the school library and I've been through the book and it's surprisingly dull. From the things I've heard about Dad, I'd have thought that he'd have chosen some racier reading. There's miles of Russian names, and chapters with headings like: "The Idiosyncrasies of the Cargle Case." I drift off the moment I start to read and have to keep reminding myself that there might be something important in there.

Although the book's truly toothgrindingly uninteresting, we do discover what a dead letter box is. It's a public place, mostly used by spies, where one person leaves a message for another. Like, tucked into a cereal packet in a supermarket, or stuck under the sugar in a café, or in the left luggage department of a station.

But it doesn't mean anything to me.

"Oh, this is hopeless," I say, handing the book to Ellie.

I pick up a comic annual and sink into a beanbag. I can't help feeling that Dad's box has been a bad thing.

I was perfectly all right before it came into my life.

Bored, perhaps, but all right, all the same.

It's been a roller coaster ever since. Not a roller coaster, maybe more of a dodgem car ride or one of those giant tea cups that make you throw up.

"But, Scarlett, look!" says Ellie. She's waving the book in my face. I can't see anything but strings of meaningless names. "This — this is a dead letter box message itself."

"Is it?" I ask.

"Look — here!" She points at page five. "...*Fundamentally*..." but the F has been underlined. Not very strongly, but definitely underlined. "And here." She turns over a couple of pages. "...*Ask yourself* ... The A?"

We scour the pages, collecting letters. F. A. Z. A. C. K. E. R. L. E. Y.

"Fazackerley?" I say. "The only Fazackerley I know of is the hall place? With the café and stuff."

It takes Ellie about a nanosecond to log on to the library computer, enter Mrs Gayton's password and get the Internet on screen.

"Fazackerley Hall," she says, typing the words in.

Pictures of a large house pop up on the screen. It's red and brick and covered in tea-shop signs and full of old people. I've been there with Mum.

"*Open daily, 10–5, located two miles from Dampmouth Bay, five miles from Dampington,*" reads Ellie. "Bingo," she says.

"How," I ask, "did *you* know Mrs Gayton's password?"

Feeling Dizzy

I'm feeling bouncy on the school bus. Ellie gets off before me, taking the dead-letter-box book (apparently it could make good bedtime reading), and although Melissa and Amber sit on the back seat singing: *"Scarlett, Scarlett, give me your answer do..."* I don't really mind.

We've made a discovery; we know more than the box does.

We know more than the mayoress and her driver.

We know where we need to go next. I'm imagining us finding a chest of secrets in the corridors of Fazackerley Hall, one that the current owners haven't noticed. They're so grateful, they share it with us, and give me a DVD that Dad made before he died, explaining everything.

The lady mayoress and her driver don't feature in this scenario at all.

I'm just getting to the bit where Dad turns out not to be dead after all.

"Uh-oh!" says the bus driver. "Trouble?"

Two police cars stand on the gravel driveway of the watercress beds. Even from here, I can see that the kitchen window's been smashed.

"Ooooooo-ooooh," screech the Coven.

But I don't answer them, because my mouth has gone dry. I clamber from the bus in silence and as I get closer to the house, I begin to feel dizzy.

There's a policeman crouching below the kitchen window, taking photos of the ground.

"Oh — scene of crime," he says. "You'll have to wait there."

"What's happened? Where's Mum?"

"Sergeant!" the policeman yells through the broken window. "There's a girl out here. Wait there, love," he says.

I stand outside the front door.

My front door.

I'm utterly numb.

I can't think.

Where's Mum?

Where's Syd?

The silence seems to last for hours. I watch the swallows swoop over the watercress beds, catching flies as if nothing's happened.

A buzzard sweeps overhead.

Then feet sound on the stairs, and Mum bursts out of the front door, closely followed by Uncle Derek. He's carrying Syd.

"Scarlett!" says Mum, rushing towards me, her arms wide. She's been crying. "We've been burgled."

I let her hold me tight. Burgled? I think of the twenty-year-old TV and the second-hand laptop. "What did they take?"

Uncle Derek lets Syd slide to the ground. "We thought you might know."

I feel suddenly sick. "Why?"

"Because it's your bedroom that's been turned upside down."

Policemen

The house smells strange. It stinks of what Mum calls "manly sweat" with low tones of policeman aftershave.

There are four policemen. One of them's Uncle Derek, one seems to be making tea and the other two are dusting everything with grey powder.

"Do you need my fingerprints?" I ask.

Uncle Derek pats me on the head. "No need, Scarlett, love – your hands are small, like Syd's, we can tell which ones belong to you."

"Upstairs, sweetheart," says Mum, behind me. She sounds oddly jolly, but I can hear a quiver in her voice, like she might cry.

My feet thunder on the stairs; the stair gate seems more awkward than usual, and the landing sad and grubby.

The door to my room's smeared with the grey powder, so I don't touch it. I just shove against it with my shoulder.

And I have to shove, because the door will barely open.

They're right. My room *has* been turned upside down.

Completely.

The bunk's lying on its head, like there's been an earthquake. The floor's centimetres deep in clothes and teddies and games. On top of them lie the books, ripped from their shelves and left for dead like broken seagulls.

I want to scream and cry at the same time, but instead I stand mutely staring at the mess.

"Scarlett?" Uncle Derek's holding my arm. "What's missing, love — what should be here that isn't?"

At first I look for electrical things. The MP3, the CD player, my camera. They're all there. The old tape player's still plugged in, but my jumble-sale tapes have gone.

Weird.

I look around, trying to remember where things were before the burglar hurricane hit them.

I remember Dad's tools, but they're in Mum's room.

They would have been under the bunk with the rest of the things from the box.

The box? Dad's photos?

I search frantically in the space where "under the bunk" should be.

I look around for the box. It's not here. It's not anywhere.

I stumble through the rubble on the floor. Combing it with my hands. I can't see any of the photos, or the book. Or even a piece of squashed cardboard.

I shake my head, tears fill my eyes; I've lost everything of Dad's, but out loud I say, "Apart from some old tapes, nothing's missing."

"Really – nothing at all, love?" asks Uncle Derek.

I shake my head again and sniff.

I've lost everything but the stupid tools.

Then I feel the key round my neck, and the library card in my pocket.

Almost everything.

"Strange," says Uncle Derek. "Strange," he says again, and clicks his stopwatch.

Oven Chips

We sleep at Uncle Derek's.

For once, I don't really mind.

Earlier, Uncle Derek cooked while Mum rang friends and cried and laughed and drank billions of cups of tea.

We had oven chips, fish fingers, frozen peas and tinned sweetcorn. It was delicious, and we all sat together round the table, with Syd in Ellie's old sparkly high chair, squeezing ketchup over everything.

It was almost as if the robbery hadn't happened.

As if we were a proper family that always ate

together, but I knew that Dad's clues were lurking in the background, that we had to do something about them, and soon.

I was trying to think of a way of asking about Fazackerley Hall, when Ellie spoke.

"D-ad?" she said.

"Yes, pumpkin." Uncle Derek grinned over the table at her.

"We need to go to Fazackerley Hall."

It wasn't the way I'd have said it. How was she going to explain a sudden interest in old buildings and tea shops?

Mum blinked. "Why?"

Exactly. Why? I stared at Ellie.

She stared back at me.

"Homework?" I said.

"A competition?" she said.

Mum and Uncle Derek gazed at us, as if we'd just turned into hamsters.

"Competition?" If Mum's eyebrows could meet in the middle, they would have done.

"Homework?" said Uncle Derek.

"Ho-wuk, 'arlet," said Syd, ploughing the ketchup with a fish finger.

"Homework." Uncle Derek gave everyone a bowl

of perfectly round pink ice cream, and whisked the fish finger out of Syd's hand. "Homework's fun, challenges the mind."

I can think of a million ways of describing homework and none of them are "fun".

"I'll take you," said Uncle Derek.

Mum touched his arm and smiled up at him. "Good idea, thank you, Derek."

And they kissed.

That was hours ago. The house is really quiet now.

Although Uncle Derek and Ellie aren't really my family, it's nice to be staying with them, having them around us. Sleeping.

Just this once.

After being burgled.

Mum and I are in Uncle Derek's big double bed, with Syd. I could have slept with Ellie, but I chose Mum, I really wanted to be with her.

I don't think anyone's properly asleep, but I feel safe. It's not very comfortable, and it smells of Uncle Derek's deodorant. He's downstairs on the sofa; he's got Houdini, our cat, for company.

We had to bring Houdini, because of all the broken glass.

I imagine Houdini's lying on Uncle Derek's head.

I lie awake listening to Syd breathing, Uncle Derek snoring downstairs, and Ellie's mass of electronic things recharging overnight.

The house hums.

Over us is a lampshade in the shape of a jellyfish. I don't suppose it's deliberately a jellyfish, but in the dark, that's what it looks like.

There are eyes, and tendrils.

I snuggle next to Mum and even though I don't want to, I think about the burglary.

I know who it is, of course.

But I can't say.

A Fine Collection
of Sugar Tongs

Mum thinks it's a good idea that we go to Fazackerly Hall. She's not coming with us, she's going home to clear up.

We're going with Syd and Uncle Derek, so we won't have to walk which makes Ellie happy, but which is going to make it more complicated.

It also means that Mum's at home on her own.

"Mum, don't go with anyone — don't get in any cars, will you?"

"Darling — what do you mean?"

"I mean, be careful — don't take lifts from strangers."

Mum laughs. "I'm supposed to say that to you, aren't I?"

She's not taking me seriously. "Please, Mum — I want you to promise me."

Mum kisses me on the forehead. "I doubt I'll even leave the house, I'll drive myself over and back. I won't need to take a lift from a stranger. Anyway, Derek's police friends will be dusting for fingerprints again today, I won't be on my own."

"Well, just make sure," I say, pulling on my trainers. "I had a sort of dream — I was worried."

"OK, love," says Mum. "I'll be extra careful."

There are about a million ancient people parked in the car park, with spotless boring cars. Uncle Derek's fits in perfectly. If Syd hadn't left smeary handprints all over the inside of the window you wouldn't know the car belonged to a comparatively young person.

Uncle Derek has one of those bobbly wooden bead seat covers like taxi drivers. He says it's ergonomically good for his back.

We follow the ancient people to the ticket office.

They take hours to go through, and Syd gets whiny and I can see Uncle Derek's just dying to run across all the lovely green lawns. I'm looking around at everything and I realise that I've no idea what I'm looking for or where I'm looking for it. Ellie raises an eyebrow at me and points at the guide book. I nod, and she slips one into Uncle Derek's hand.

"Seventeen quid?" he yelps, when the woman gives him three tickets.

"Well, sir, the guidebook's three pounds fifty and the house does have the finest collection of weighing scales in the country."

"Not to mention the East Wing," says a passing guide.

Uncle Derek looks at us. "Are you sure about this?"

Ellie nods firmly. "We've got to go because of homework, and we need the book for the same reason."

She's turning into an excellent liar.

The house is gobsmackingly dull. The room of eighteenth-century weighing scales is especially boring. But we have to examine everything. Looking for notes, or keyholes, or anywhere Dad could have left a message.

Ellie looks interested in everything, but it could just be a ruse. Syd rubs slime over the tapestries and demands ice creams.

Uncle Derek gets trapped in a room with a guide determined to show him every one of the fine collection of sugar tongs.

"Girls," says Uncle Derek, fighting his way to the door. "Haven't we done enough?"

"But we haven't done the East Wing," Ellie says, thwacking the guidebook against her thigh. Neither of us have read a single word from it.

"No," Uncle Derek sighs. "We haven't." We all look at Syd. He's lolling out of his pushchair singing "Incy Wincy Spider" over and over again in a high squeak. "Tell you what, I'll take Sydney here out in the gardens, we can run around, have an ice cream." He looks at his watch. "See you in thirty-two minutes."

"OK, Dad," says Ellie.

Pale Green
Eyeshadow

But it doesn't work that way, because a second later, Uncle Derek's phone rings and he's called away to a suspicious fire on the other side of town.

"Girls, I'm really sorry, I can either rush you back now, or leave you here?"

"We'll stay," we chorus.

"Well, if you're sure?" Uncle Derek looks worried and relieved all at once. "How will you get back?"

"Bus," says Ellie at the same time as I say, "Walk."

"Well, don't take any lifts from strangers and here's a fiver for cake or tea or something."

In the end, we keep Syd too. Uncle Derek drives

off with a blue flashing light on the top of his car.

We get to the entrance of the East Wing, with Syd in his pushchair, two backpacks and our tickets.

"Oh, no, no – you really can't bring that in here. Where are your parents?" He's a whiskery man in a hot tweed suit. He looks like he'd rather be at home watching the cricket than here dealing with people like us.

"We're on our own," I say.

"But my dad's a policeman," says Ellie.

"I don't care if your dad's the Queen." He points to Syd. "You're not bringing that in here, in that state."

I look at Syd. He's licking his palms. They're the cleanest part of him.

"Look." The man crouches, he probably thinks he's more charming like that but he's not, he's just less tall. "There's a block of lavatories over there, with some lockers. You can leave all your paraphernalia in one of those, wash that..." he points at Syd, "and perhaps I'll let you in next time."

"Pooh," says Ellie as we trek towards the toilets.

I think of a much ruder collection of words.

"Do you think it's in the East Wing?" says Ellie.

"I don't know where it is — I wish I knew what we were even looking for." My dreams of trunks of secrets have crashed in flames. I'd quite like us to go home before I die of heritage boredom.

"We're looking for diamonds, silly," says Ellie, picking a stone from the side of her shoe.

"Are we?" We may, sort of, be looking for diamonds, but I think I'm still looking for Dad.

"Poo?" says Syd hopefully and breaks out of his pushchair.

We chase him outside, over the grass, through the old people with their cups and saucers, and out on to the drive. He can move really fast when he wants to, and I'm pushing a pushchair, and Ellie's got the backpacks.

"Syd!" I yell and I'm about to lunge for him, but a movement catches my eye.

It's them. They're here, the lady mayoress and the chauffeur.

I stop, and Syd stops because I'm not chasing him, and Ellie chugs up behind.

"What?" she says, bent double and panting like a dog.

I lean over next to her. "It's them. Don't look

now, but they're over by the tea shop."

"The café?" Ellie jerks up her head.

"It's all right, they can't do anything here," I say. "It's too public."

"But how did they know *we* were here?" Ellie looks worried.

I think about the letter-boxes book, but that's still safely at Ellie's house and it was the only thing that led us here. "They must have followed us."

"Now that," Ellie says, "is creepy."

She uncurls and we amble towards Syd. I'm trying not to look towards the tea shop, but I do want to see what they're up to.

The man's not wearing the grey suit now. He's got a sweaty blue shirt on instead. He's balancing a tray of tea and scones, and jam and milk, and stumbling through the tables. His teapot's sprinkling the old ladies with trails of boiling water. It's causing a rumpus.

Up at the far end of the tea garden, the lady mayoress is applying make-up from a sparkly purple bag. She's got a tiny mirror, and I bet she's watching us. Her face is kind of orange with pale green eyeshadow and crimson lipstick. Her enormous bottom flows over the sides of the little wooden chair and I can't help thinking of what Ellie said. She does look like a Christmas bauble, and everyone around her looks as dull and brown as a fir cone.

I try to pretend I haven't noticed them, so I stroll by, casually tracking Syd, who of course has no idea what's going on. Ellie follows, and Syd instantly makes a run for it the moment he knows he's got our attention.

Luckily, he doesn't head for the café, instead, he doubles back towards the toilet block and it takes us five precious minutes to corner him. He runs into the gents then runs out screaming, "Stinky!" and I tackle him by the tall bank of lockers.

"'Arlet," he says, slipping his fingers up my nose when I've finally got him clamped in my arms.

"Syd," I say. "Time to go."

He reaches his little fingers up to my throat. He pulls on the key until it falls out of my T-shirt. It clinks on the concrete floor.

It looks exactly like a locker key.

The Last
Raspberry Sherbet

"Which one?" asks Ellie.

There are hundreds of lockers, and I'm thinking that it's only a matter of seconds before the driver comes to find us.

I finger the key as if it could home in on the right locker. Gripping Syd by the wrist I stand up, and think through the things in the box. *Come on, Dad, which one?* And then I remember the book, *Gone with the Wind.*

"Number thirty-nine," I say, walking over to stick the key into the lock.

Whoa. It fits.

It turns, smoothly, and I pull the door open, keeping my eyes closed. Is this going to be another of his disappointments?

"What is *that*?" says Ellie, loudly, next to me.

I open my eyes. Inside, wedged against the back of the locker is a rough bundle of paper trussed in elastic bands. We might have expected something like that, but attached to the bundle by a sagging red string is what looks like a battered, old-fashioned Airfix kit.

I grab both, and fighting the urge to rip them open, stuff them in my backpack.

"That's it, then," Ellie says. "Let's run."

"Poo," says Syd. "I sc-ream."

"NO!" Ellie and I shout, together.

Ellie shoulders the backpacks while I strap Syd into the pushchair.

"I SCREAM!" yells Syd, just as I stick my nose round the corner of the toilet block. The note is spine-shatteringly loud.

"Can't you shut him up?" says Ellie.

Panicking, I reach into my jeans. I've still got a single stolen sherbet raspberry welded to the paper bag, and a fizzing snake spotted with pocket fluff. "Here." I stuff them into Syd's clammy hand, and at a fast walk, head out of the toilet block towards the main gate.

"Bus?" asks Ellie hopefully.

"Walk; we can head off over the footpath. Otherwise we'll be stuck on the side of the road for ages. They'll get us."

The lady mayoress is pretending to be interested in scones, but the pair of them are perfectly lined up for the gateway. There's no way we can get past without being spotted.

Rats.

"We'll have to go another way," I say, dragging the pushchair backwards across the gravel.

"Try the back of the house?" says Ellie. There's panic in her voice.

I expect there's panic in mine.

The grumpy man in the tweed suit's sneaking a pork pie as we creep past him. He doesn't seem to notice us, although he stands up and wipes his glasses with a handkerchief and afterwards peers closely at the ruts the pushchair leaves in the gravel.

We turn right into a courtyard, by a log pile. The walls are high but not impossible to climb. At least, not for me.

Ellie's wearing a stupid little blue flowery skirt.

Not ideal for this.

Not ideal for anything.

I can see it's going to be tricky to get her over the wall, especially as it's a scratchy, mossy, leafy, mouldy sort of a wall with a crumbly top.

"How are we going to get out?" she asks, looking at the wall as if it's going to eat her. She's almost in tears.

"Easy." I stand on a log and peer over. Fields and hedges run towards Dampmouth Bay. "We can get home this way. Go on – you first," I say. "Then I'll hand you the pushchair."

"But I can't do that!" Ellie looks at the wall, completely terrified.

"I'll give you a leg up."

"It's all icky, Scarlett." She's got her most pathetic voice out now. The one that puts smiley faces over all the "i"s.

"Ellie – come on!" I shout. "Would you rather get icky or get caught by those two?"

I hold my hand out, like a stirrup, and she lands her clean pink sandal in my palm.

"I don't want to do this, Scarlett," she says. "It's only because you're my friend."

I look up at her watery eyes behind the ridiculous

glasses. Friend? I suppose it goes both ways now. I need her as much as she needs me. "I don't want to do it either, let's just get it over with. Put your hand on my head, the other on the wall."

She does, and I give her a massive shove, scraping her leg right up the side until she topples over the top of the wall.

"Ow!" she squeals.

"What?" I've got Syd by the wrist, and I'm trying to work out the fox, sheep, lettuce, slug, duck thing, again. Should I send the pushchair over or Syd?

"Nettles, thousands of them – I've stung my bum," Ellie whines. "And there's cow poo over here."

I take Syd from the pushchair, and clamp him between my knees.

Ellie's still moaning on the other side of the wall, but I can hear footsteps on the gravel, someone's moving around on our side of the house.

"Here comes the pushchair." I stuff it over the wall and hear it crash in the nettles.

"Ow!" says Ellie again. "Stung my hand."

"Sorry," I say. "And Syd." I stand on the log and lift him over the wall.

He puts his feet on the top and looks as if he's going to make a run for it along the shaky brickwork.

"No, you don't!" shouts Ellie, and he disappears. There's a thump and Syd squeals, and I hear the strap of the pushchair click shut. "Ha!"

Now, there's just me.

I look around for another log, and peeking through a bush that screens the corner of the courtyard, I see that the chauffeur's deep in conversation with the grumpy tweedy man. He's pointing in our direction.

Rats.

The logs are all too uneven to stack. I need something to spring from, to give me a leg up. But all I can find is a wheelbarrow, so I take it over to the wall and climb in.

Although I can nearly stretch my foot to the top of the wall, I just can't quite get up there.

Rats and double rats.

I'm going to have to pretend it's a vaulting horse.

I turn the wheelbarrow over, so that it's leaning against the wall.

"Over here, I should think, the scamps." It's the tweedy man, he's bringing them our way. "Are you a policeman, sir? The little girl said her father was a policeman."

I make myself breathe.

"Oh, yes, CID, you know, hush-hush," says the chauffeur. He's definitely this side of the house. "Protecting the good lady here."

"Fascinating, fascinating." The tweedy man's voice is getting closer.

They already know we're here somewhere, so I take a chance and step out from the bush to give myself a longer run-up.

"There!" shouts the tweedy man.

"I see her!" says the lady mayoress. "Scarlett — lovey."

They're all running now.

"OK, Scarlett," I say to myself. "You can do it."

I take one skip and then in three long strides, my legs motor towards the wheelbarrow. One foot lands firmly on the underside of the barrow and as it starts to collapse, I throw my body forward so that my hands hold the top of the wall, and the rest of my body follows in a messy half-flip half-vault.

The wall vanishes beneath me and I kick my feet as I go over, so that I land, already running, beyond the nettles. Ellie's halfway across the field, struggling with the pushchair, Syd screaming every step of the way.

"Hey!" shouts a man behind me. Chauffeur?

"Come back," shouts another. Tweed?

But we seem to have developed wings.

Hu-pty Du-pty

It all starts to fall apart by the time we reach the second field. Ellie complains about the heat and cow poo and thistles. Syd just complains.

He mostly complains by singing. "Hu-pty Du-pty, sat on the wall," except he only knows one line, so Humpty Dumpty never actually falls off.

At least the penguins couldn't sing.

"Can't you make him stop?" says Ellie again.

I grab a handful of dandelion seed heads and Syd mashes them, but it only shuts him up for a millisecond.

We stumble on.

Ellie's given me the pushchair. I can see why she doesn't want it; it's rubbish at fields and rocks and mud, the wheels are tiny and jammed up with green stuff.

This is not a good way to make an escape.

I stop to clear the wheels. Syd crumbles dandelion seeds down the back of my neck.

I look back. There's no way that woman would make it over the wall, no matter how many tweedy men helped her. But I'm not so sure about her friend the chauffeur. He could be just behind the hedge, watching us.

"Come on, Ellie – one last run."

"Scarlett, can't we stop for a minute?"

But she follows.

We run into town and duck through the streets all the way back to Ellie's house; it's nearer than mine.

"What if your dad's not back?" I shout.

But he is. He opens the door just as we arrive. "I wondered what had happened to you! I was coming to have a look."

He stares at us. Syd's wailing and tearful and his pushchair's sprouted most of a hedgerow. Ellie's not much better. Her legs have gone red and blotchy, except for all the little white stinging nettle rings, and she's got leaves in her hair.

Her perfect pink sandals aren't perfect any more. They're not really pink either. More cow poo.

"What?" says Uncle Derek.

"We got lost," I say quickly.

"We thought we'd take a short cut," says Ellie.

"Had a g-ate fall," says Syd.

The Scrapbook

Syd's downstairs watching the cartoon channel with Uncle Derek. They're eating iced buns with jam inside. Uncle Derek'll wish he hadn't had that idea once Syd wipes his hands on the sofa.

The white sofa.

We're in Ellie's bedroom, but it wasn't easy getting up here. Uncle Derek kept asking questions and picking mud off our shoes, and staring at us in a meaningful way. But Ellie held her nerve and I said nothing, and Syd hadn't a clue what had happened, so now we've got the papers we took from the locker open on the floor. A scrapbook, that's what it is. Sheets of black paper plastered with pictures and newspaper cuttings, going right back to 1985.

There are also other things. Pretty labels, beer mats, stamps, packaging from other countries. I flick through without reading it, just soaking in the pictures.

A bill from a restaurant stops me. *Margarita pizza with extra olives, mushrooms and capers.* That's what I always have.

Weird.

There's a receipt for twelve pairs of black socks. I screw up my eyes, and despite Ellie's bedroom, I can almost see Dad. He *did* always wear black socks. Black socks with brown shoes.

I hold my breath so that I can't smell the soap powder, and try harder.

I get a glimpse of him sailing in through our front door. He's holding a bunch of flowers, yellow ones, all wrapped in gorgeous white lacy cellophane, and I can almost smell them. He's wearing the brown shoes, the jacket, the jeans, and he's smiling. Maybe he's even laughing. His hair's acting like a halo, curly, lit by the sun outside, but I can see his eyes, bright and surprising in his dark face.

He says something I can't quite hear, but I can

feel my own excitement. I've been looking forward to this; it might even be my birthday. Mum charges in from the side of the picture and they hug, and the whole memory's flooded with sunlight.

And then it's gone.

And I feel happy and sad, all at once. It was as if he was here, and I try to get back to the memory, get Dad back in the room, but he won't come, so I go back to the scrapbook.

On another page, there's a wrapper for a Cornish pasty. It's made of brown paper, slightly greasy. Next to it are three tickets, little green tear-off tickets, for a ferry in Cornwall. Two adults and a child.

I rub my forefinger over them. They're flat now, but they were once curly, because they come out of one of those ancient ticket machines that makes the clicky bicycle sound. I close my eyes to listen. The man turns the handle twice for each ticket and I'm back by a triangle of water, caught between black overhanging branches. I'm looking up, as if I'm in a pushchair. I can see Mum's duffle coat, and Dad's legs, and I'm cold and there's an engine, shaking under my feet. It smells of oil, and sea, and pasty.

"Whoa, look at this," shouts Ellie.

I jump. I'm back in Ellie's stinky bedroom with piles of soft toys and pink cushions.

She's jabbing the scrapbook, pointing at a large newspaper cutting.

"Scarlett, look!"

My eyes run over the words but I don't take them in. "Emerald" and "gangsters" are hard to ignore, but I'm not very interested. I'm interested in the bits of Dad that Dad's left in the scrapbook. The pieces that trigger a real moment of Dad, and that can tell me more about him as a person.

Just at the moment, I don't want him to be a spy.

But Ellie does.

"Listen, if you won't read: *'The Fedora Emerald, the fifth largest ever found, flawless in every way, is tonight back in the safe-keeping of the Queen's Royal Treasury. Believed stolen during the Second World War, when it was removed for cleaning, rumours have placed it in Berlin, Paris, Rome and Moscow, until it disappeared completely in 1980. Eventually, the emerald was believed to have found its way to Uzbekistani gangsters, in payment for arms. However sources close to the treasury say that a covert operation has recovered the jewel, and it is now to be kept in London under armed guard.'* That's your dad."

"How do you know? He might have had nothing to do with it," I say, destroying the pile of teddies.

"Why else would he have it?" Ellie says. "You don't keep press cuttings of other people's successes, do you? I mean, my dad only cuts out things from the paper that relate to us."

I shrug. It sounds like something from a fairy tale, not real life. I run my fingers over the ferry tickets. They're from real life.

"And this," says Ellie. " *'The documents stolen from the Home Secretary's briefcase last month have been discovered in a Whitehall office. Although government sources are trying to play down the contents of the documents, it is believed that they were of great importance to national security. When asked about the find in the Whitehall office, the government spokesman declined to comment.'* "

"OK — so he stole things back," I say. "We already knew that — your dad told us."

"Yes — but this is proof, proof that he did the right thing; that he wasn't doing it for personal gain."

"So?"

When You Lie, Which Way Do Your Eyes Go?

I can't help feeling dismal. I keep looking at the scrapbook, looking for more about Dad. I want him to have written something personal, something for me. But this was for him.

So far as I can see, there's nothing about it we need to keep secret, so I take it downstairs when Mum comes back and put it on Uncle Derek's spotless table.

"Oh, Scarlett, I've never seen this before, how fantastic. Where on earth did it come from?" says Mum, picking through the pages, laughing at the restaurant bill, rubbing her fingers over the sock receipt as if she could get closer to him too. She looks up at me, her eyes all watery. "Where did you get it, Scarlett?"

I hadn't thought of that.

I stare at Ellie – she can't help me, she stares back, her shoulders rising into a silent shrug.

A flash of inspiration: "It came with the tools, Dad's solicitor brought it."

I wait, holding my breath, for Mum to ask the next question.

"So, why didn't you show it to me? Why didn't you say?"

Ellie nudges me.

"I – forgot?"

Both Mum and Uncle Derek stop looking at the scrapbook and look up at me instead. When you lie, I think your eyes go to the left – so I make mine go to the right. I hope it doesn't look too obvious.

There's this epic silence. Even the fly on the window's stopped buzzing to have a listen.

"Surely you couldn't forget something like this?" says Mum. "It's got such a lot of your dad in it."

I don't know the answer to that one so I say, "I don't know what I was thinking."

"Oh look," says Mum. "One of the prison

postcards." She gazes at a picture of Dampmouth lifeboat. It's addressed to Wormwood Scrubs Prison. "I used to imagine some civil servant picking them up from the prison and popping them in an airmail envelope – sending them away to your dad."

"Why?" I ask.

"Because it was how we kept in touch – messages back and forth – a comfort, I suppose. Without the postcards, I'd not have been able to contact him at all."

"Oh…" I say, feeling Uncle Derek's eyes staring into the top of my head. He's probably re-living the conversation where he told us Dad was a spy, and wondering just how much I did or didn't know. He probably looks just like a plain-clothes policeman solving a crime, but I daren't look up to see.

Ellie coughs and starts stroking Houdini like her life depends on it.

"Hmm," says Mum, turning to another page in the scrapbook. "Oh – I remember that," she says, pointing to the article about the Fedora Emerald. "And the documents; they'd got as far as Berlin as I remember."

"Look, there," Uncle Derek says, pointing at a

page near the end. He's got a funny expression on his face. It might be because he thinks I'm lying, but it could be that this is the first time Dad's really been around us and perhaps he doesn't like it.

"What am I looking at?" asks Mum.

" '*The Moonshine Children's Holiday Club received an anonymous gift of five hundred thousand pounds*...blah di blah ... *a spokesman* ... blah di blah ... *no idea where it came from* ... *left in cash on the doorstep.*' "

Mum's face crinkles into a frown. She looks up at Uncle Derek, but he's still searching the scrapbook.

"And this little one — '*Mr Eustace Golden, war hero, aged eighty-nine, can now rest safe in his house, as an anonymous donor has secured the financial future of the street, funding essential repair works to all the houses*... blah, blah...*doorstep in cash.*' "

"What?" says Ellie.

"And here..."

Mum interrupts. "... *Happy Hedgehogs, the wild animal sanctuary on Exmoor, threatened with its own extinction, is now celebrating the gift of two hundred and fifty thousand pounds to allow the renovation and expansion of the existing buildings* .... blah, blah ... *suitcase on the doorstep.*' '

"Blimey," says Uncle Derek, reaching into the fridge for a bowl of perfectly sliced carrot sticks.

"Blimey, suitcases, eh? Blimey."

"So," asks Ellie, "are you saying that Scarlett's dad gave money away?"

Mum nods. I don't think she can open her mouth, or she'd cry, but Uncle Derek has no problem.

"That's it – that's what it was all about," he says. "All that diamond stuff, all that secrecy? And he was just selling them, and giving away the money. No wonder they never found any diamonds – there weren't any, not after ... he..." Uncle Derek looks uncomfortable – he can't actually say "died".

"He didn't just give it away, he gave it to good causes," says Ellie, peering at the scrapbook over Mum's shoulder.

"Exactly – I mean, what a thing to do!" Uncle Derek shakes his head and pops a carrot stick into his mouth. "You've got to admire the man, terrifying way to raise money for charity. I mean, I've raised five hundred quid from the marathons, and they're hard work, but this – this is a completely different league."

He chomps on the carrot and little orange chunks work their way out on to his moustache. But he doesn't notice because he's thinking.

I look at Ellie. I suspect we're both thinking

about the chauffeur. "What about the people who were after him — you said something about the Queenie gang? London gangster types. What are they looking for?"

"Were," says Uncle Derek. "Very much were. They're nearly all behind bars, except for Queenie and her brother, couldn't actually pin anything on those two — they *were* after the diamonds."

"But they don't exist any more," says Ellie. "Scarlett's dad sold them."

"Exactly," says Uncle Derek. "That'll be why they gave up, stopped chasing after Scarlett and Carole."

"I wonder," says Ellie very quietly to Houdini. Houdini looks back up at her and sinks his claws into her pink slippers.

"Yow!" squeals Ellie.

"Well, it's wonderful," says Mum. "I'm so glad you've got this, Scarlett — it's so nice to have something of his."

"Hmmm," says Uncle Derek. I'm sure he's watching my eyes, so I look away and stare at the book.

He doles perfectly formed balls of pink ice cream into matching bowls.

Mum's turning the pages. I start to count; six, seven, eight cases of sudden gifts to charities. Nine, ten, there are millions of them. He must have given away thousands and thousands, but surely, Dad didn't do all that, just to give it away? Uncle Derek's right, it's a ridiculously hard way to raise money for charity, surely anyone would make tea and cakes and sell second-hand clothes rather than climb in and out of high-security buildings under CCTV cameras and submachine guns?

Surely.

Uncle Derek hands me a bowl of ice cream.

Perhaps Dad liked the risk?

Perhaps he wanted me to do good deeds too and that's why he left me the tools and the box and the scrapbook. Not for running around rescuing penguins, but something else.

He obviously didn't leave me the diamonds. I know I shouldn't, but I do feel slightly disappointed that he sold them all.

It would have been so lovely.

Then I think about the key and the clues – why didn't he just leave me the scrapbook, or give it to Mum to give me. Why go to so much trouble?

I take a mouthful of pink ice cream and let the

cold freeze my tongue.

Why leave messages all over the place? He could have told Mum, and she could have told me; after all, it's something to be proud of. She could have told me to keep looking up, and she's made me keep up the gym.

I take another bite of the ice cream and it squeaks against my teeth.

Or is he trying to test me in some way? Only the worthy get the prize – but if the prize is a scrapbook, why make it so secretive?

I think about the mayoress and the chauffeur. They're after the diamonds, they wouldn't want anything else, so they must think they still exist. Dad waited to give me the box until I was eleven, because he must have hoped that they'd have given up by then. But if there are no diamonds left, why are they after them?

This is all too much – perhaps I should just tell Uncle Derek about the lady mayoress and give up on Dad's clues? It would be the sensible thing to do.

But then Dad wasn't sensible and nor am I.

I press my fingers into my eye sockets.

"Are you all right, Scarlett?" asks Ellie, scraping a huge blob of ice cream off her chin.

Double Pike
Back Somersault

The whole school goes swimming on Wednesday. For once, they've got it right, because the weather's planning on being gorgeous.

Although we're near the sea, we go to the Dampmouth Bay Golden Jubilee Memorial Lido, which is actually in Dampmouth Sands. Dampmouth Sands makes Dampmouth Bay look really interesting, because apart from the lido all it has is a bouncy castle on the sea front that's spotted with mildew and smells of fridges.

Despite Dampmouth Sands, I like the lido. Ellie and I did a lifesaving course there last half-term.

Uncle Derek made us, in case we fell in the big tank behind the watercress beds. I'll never need to use it but I did quite enjoy diving in after a brick wearing a pair of pyjamas. It seems a funny test, though. As Ellie said: "Who needs to rescue a brick in the middle of the night?"

The lady mayoress has come swimming too. Although I can't see the car anywhere, it's definitely her; an enormous orange-skinned woman in a massive lime-green bathing suit. She's torturing a deckchair right next to the lifeguard.

I can't see the driver, and then I spot him, right at the top of the lido, watching us. I try not to look bothered. The only good thing about having them here is that I know they can't be following Syd and Mum.

Mrs Gayton stands on the side and makes us swim up and down for a century, while Mrs Mason sits in a deckchair, reading a magazine called *Practical Punctuation*.

I've done my fifteen lengths of breaststroke, and I'm hanging on the side of the pool waiting for everyone else. Ellie pants in behind me, she's a good swimmer, and we both loll, watching Melissa, Jessica and Amber struggle at the back.

I have to say, I *do* like to see them struggle.

"How many lengths have you girls done?" Mrs Gayton asks them.

Melissa and Jessica exchange glances. "Fourteen, miss?" says Jessica. Amber's too out of breath to speak.

"Rubbish," whispers Ellie. "They've only done about three."

Mrs Gayton twists her mouth round as if she doesn't completely believe them, but waits until they've done what they say is the last length and blows one of her many whistles. She's wearing her army shorts again, and big white flip flops that show off her bunions. "Right. Out of the pool. Diving next."

"Oh," Melissa and Jessica simper. "Do we *have* to do it, miss?"

For a second I think Mrs Gayton's going to let them off, but Mrs Mason looks over her magazine. "You must try it, girls. If you don't try now, you never will."

Yes!

I do my best not to laugh as Jessica pancakes from the board, her body slapping the water like a wet pitta bread. Melissa follows, completely fails to dive and jumps with her arms bent over her head. Amber bottles out, and says her foot hurts. It's not cool.

"Don't worry, girls," says Mrs Gayton. "Diving can be difficult to master at first; I remember my most challenging diving competition, twenty-foot board, double pike back somersault with half-twist and a rip entry." Mrs Gayton slaps her hand against her thigh. "Fabulous. I was fabulous."

I try to imagine Mrs Gayton in her swimsuit, looking young and springy. But I can't.

Melissa and Jessica sit on the side of the board and look ever so slightly unconfident as a line of boys hurl themselves over the side of the pool.

When it comes to Ellie's turn, she does a neat little dive, barely splashing.

Mrs Gayton ignores her.

I've ended up at the back of the queue. Mrs Gayton keeps waving people in front of me. Even Sam Lewis gets to go first. He springs miles into the air and plummets like a sea bird to the bottom of the pool. Mrs Gayton sniffs, and looks at her watch.

I'm about to do my dive when a wall of water crashes over the side of the pool. I stare, trying to make sense of what's happened. Everyone's facing the lido, gazing at a vast green flower that seems to have appeared in the middle.

It's the lady mayoress. Her skirt's pretending to be a lily pad and the rest of her makes a good frog.

There's a kind of embarrassed silence, and the boys start laughing. Mrs Gayton throws them a sharp look, then prods me.

"Scarlett? Dive. Now."

I compose myself on the side of the pool, imagining that my legs are glued together at the knee, and that my toes must be absolutely the last thing to enter the pool. The dive is pretty nearly perfect. The water presses in on me and with my eyes closed I follow my arms up to the surface. I'm enjoying the depth and that feeling of being forced up through the water, so I take my time and emerge only to see Mrs Gayton's flip flops, with Mrs Gayton's feet still inside them, disappearing into the pool.

"What?" shouts Mrs Mason from the side. Sam Lewis piles into his mates and hides, they're all of them falling apart with giggles.

"She fell in," says Sam, pointing at the pool. "She just slipped."

We stare into the water. All I can see are millions of bubbles and Mrs Gayton's tracksuit top billowing through them.

But Mrs Gayton doesn't come up.

The lifeguard's not looking, he's texting someone on his mobile phone.

Mrs Gayton still doesn't come up.

"Do something, someone!" says Mrs Mason, pulling off her cardigan.

The boys start to look anxious and move towards the fence. Melissa and Jessica gaze into the water as if something vaguely interesting was happening in a fish tank.

No one's going to do anything.

I even look up at the chauffeur, but he's eating sandwiches and fiddling with his mobile. The lady mayoress wallows on the steps at the end of the pool; she's not going to rush to save Mrs Gayton.

Am I?

Mrs Gayton, the most horrible teacher in the South of England?

Mrs Gayton – alien paratrooper?

Mrs Gayton – bully?

"Ellie!" I shout. "We'd better..."

And she dives in. I duck dive behind her and

push my way to the bottom of the pool.

Mrs Gayton's sitting down there, her eyes wide open, flapping her arms at us. I grab one side, Ellie grabs the other, and together we push up from the bottom of the pool, but Mrs Gayton's heavy and she doesn't seem to have any idea how to get up to the top.

She's not really like a brick. More like a pallet load of bricks.

There's a trail of bubbles coming out of Ellie's mouth, there's probably a trail coming out of mine. I don't know about her but I'm running out of breath. I reach out to Mrs Gayton's old chicken legs and pinch her just above the knee.

Whoa, it works – she kicks out against the bottom of the pool, and with Ellie and me pulling like crazy, we drag her to the surface.

The lifeguard's arms reach in and pull at the mass of whistles around Mrs Gayton's neck. It's one way to rescue her, and we pop out a millisecond before Mrs Gayton does.

"Whoa!" shouts Ellie.

But I'm too out of breath to say anything.

Mrs Gayton Is Not Really a Human Being

The thing is, it turns out Mrs Gayton can't swim.

We know that because we saw her sink to the bottom of the pool. Everything else is rumour. On the bus on the way back to school, everyone's telling stories of things their mums and dads have said.

Apparently:

"Mrs Gayton's husband emigrated to Australia the day after they married."

"At the weekends, Mrs Gayton's one of the wrestlers on the pier."

"Mrs Gayton's not really a human being, she's

from a computer game."

"Mrs Gayton's mum was Godzilla."

"Mrs Gayton's really a man."

Whatever's the truth, we don't see her afterwards. Instead, Mrs Mason takes our class.

I'm probably dead and gone to heaven, because for the rest of the day, Mrs Mason lets us draw all over our literacy books, and write poems about the sea.

Feeling like I'm in a dream, Ellie and I catch the school bus to her house. We sit right in the middle of the bus and no one makes fun of Ellie. Amber actually shifts along to make room.

The others have left a sort of ring around us, not the usual "you stink" kind of ring, but a ring of awe.

They're looking at us, smiling at us; but a little bit scared of us, too.

It's as if without Mrs Gayton, the Coven can't exist.

It's very nice.

That's the upside; the downside is the long black car with a little flag on the front that follows us all the way home.

We watch it slide around corner after corner just far enough away, but with no chance of losing it.

"Ellie!" shouts the bus driver. "Your stop."

We have to get out at Ellie's, the driver won't let us stay on, but before the bus has even pulled away, we duck down an alley and run all the way through the golf course until we can get back into the other end of Ellie's avenue of very neat houses.

"Phew," says Ellie, unlocking the front door. "Lost them. What a day."

But behind us, I hear the low purring of a car rolling slowly into the street. We throw ourselves in through the door and slam it shut.

I peer through the square of glass in the front door.

My mouth goes dry.

The nose of the big black car nudges the bushes at the edge of the drive and it rolls to a stop outside the house.

Mum and Syd clamber out.

"Oh no," I say.

"Oh!" Ellie gasps, ducking out of sight.

I watch Mum lean in through the car window.

"NO," I say.

"What?" asks Ellie.

"She's inviting them in."

"She can't," says Ellie.

The lady mayoress staggers out of the back of the car and up the steps towards the front door.

"NO! Absolutely not," shouts Ellie and bolts for the stairs.

The chauffeur follows from the car and Mum fiddles about in her handbag looking for her keys.

I hesitate for a moment too long.

The door opens.

"Oh – hello, dear," says the lady mayoress. "How lovely, are you going to join us for tea too?"

Mum's busy in the kitchen. I can hear cups rattling on saucers. The lady mayoress has settled herself on Uncle Derek's tilty chair. She's playing with the buttons and the foot rest keeps going up and down. Her sausage legs are going up and down with it. It's not a nice sight and it's making me nervous.

At my feet, the chauffeur's playing with Syd. Syd's running a car over the chauffeur's jacket. It's as if he knows the man as well as he knows Uncle Derek. The chauffeur gives Syd an awkward hug. Syd grips the chauffeur's jacket and buries his head in it.

Syd's really happy.

I'm not. I wish they'd go away and I don't know what to do with myself. I tried to hide in the kitchen but Mum sent me out. "Entertain them," she said, handing me a plate of Jammie Dodgers.

Between chair rides, the lady mayoress examines the room. Her eyes slide from the piano to the sound system to the lampshades. She fingers the cloth of the cushions as if she's working out how much they're worth.

Mum's still clanking about in the kitchen, so I stare at the floor. It's not very interesting; Uncle Derek doesn't really go in for interesting. It's just beige, but the chauffeur's definitely trying to catch my eye, and I'm trying really hard not to let it get caught.

In fact, I'm staring at the floor so hard, I almost don't hear him. "Scarlett," he says quietly. "Time's runnin' out."

I look up. I don't mean to and I catch Syd planting a slobbery kiss on the chauffeur's chin.

Syd loves him.

There's nothing I can do, my blood's already frozen; I can practically hear it stopping my heart.

"Syd," I mutter.

"Well, Scarlett, dear?" asks the lady mayoress.

"Syd, come here." I hold out my hand but Syd burrows closer to the chauffeur.

The lady mayoress leans forward. "All right, ducks? Be lovely if you decided to help us, save a lot of bother."

I suddenly remember the biscuits.

"Syd," I say. "Biscuit?" I hold out the plate.

"Ta, love," says the lady mayoress, grabbing one with her painted nails and jamming it into her mouth.

Syd gazes up at the chauffeur's face, then looks ravenously at the plate of biscuits. He uncurls from the man's chest, launches himself across the room towards me and snatches a biscuit before rolling off behind the telly to eat it.

Phew.

"Thing is, Scarlett, dear," says the lady mayoress. "We saw you'd had a present, a box, but when we 'learned' about the contents, they were ... disappointing."

The chauffeur's up on his feet now, turning over the books on the piano stool, flicking through the magazines on the coffee table, poking about.

He moves over to my school bag, picks up one of

the straps and looks me in the eye.

The scrapbook's in there.

I try to look as if it doesn't matter, make myself breathe.

I try to breathe like a normal person, but my heartbeat's going mad in my ears and I don't feel a bit normal.

I shrug.

"Knowing our criminal friend, as we did," says the chauffeur, passing the strap through his fingers. "We know, and you know, that there's something else out there, something that belongs to us. You've a choice — you can either give us everything you know, now — and we'll be out of your lives forever, or have us follow you, until you lead us there. It could take years — but then, we've already waited five."

He swings my school bag from one finger, watching me closely. "Worried I might find somethin'?" he mutters, reaching for the zip.

"Go on, dearie, do make it simple," says the lady mayoress.

"Yes," says the chauffeur. "Don't be a spoilsport, Scarlett — I'd hate to wreck your mum's summer holiday." He steps across the carpet until he's towering over me, the bag dangling from his hand.

I take a step back. I want the bag but I don't want to be next to the man. I try to remember what else is in there. He'll have to sort through loads of old rubbish to find the scrapbook. He won't just reach in and pull it out.

But then again...

"Mum!" I squeak.

" 'Um!" bellows Syd. " 'Artlet want -ooo."

Mum bursts in with the tea tray. "Ready for a cup?"

The room fills with movement and the sound of shiny fabric bouncing back into place. Still holding the bag, the driver leaps forward and hauls the lady mayoress to her feet.

"Must go," he says. "Places to go, people to see."

"But, Mum!" I say. "He's got my bag."

Mum lands the tea tray on the coffee table and stares at the chauffeur and me. "I don't understand," she says.

"That was lovely, dear," says the lady mayoress, a beach load of crumbs cascading from her stomach to the carpet.

"You're going without a cup of tea?" says Mum.

"Oh, thank you, the biscuits were most restorative,

dearie," says the lady mayoress. "And I nearly forgot." She rustles in her handbag and pulls out a bag of boiled sweets. "Here, lovey." She presses a glowing red sweet into Syd's hand. "For you, petal." Syd beams. He'd go anywhere with these two.

"Er – excuse me, you've got Scarlett's bag?" Mum says, hesitating in the doorway, but the chauffeur ignores her.

Outside, the lady mayoress lurches towards the car, her heels sticking in the gaps in Uncle Derek's drive. The chauffeur, behind, winks at me, and he's just about to swing my bag into the car when I bound forward and grab it off him.

He stares at me.

I stare back.

"Oh," says Mum. "Good, you've got it back now, Scarlett." But she's speaking slowly as if she's trying to make sense of their behaviour.

"So she has," he laughs. "How did that happen? Lovely to see you again – Scarlett."

I don't answer, but looping the bag over my shoulder, I hang on to Mum's shirt, just to keep her there, with me. I've forgotten about Syd, because he charges out between Mum's legs to stroke the car one more time. "Whoa there, little fella," says the chauffeur and he picks Syd up and throws him into the air above his head.

It's too high. Far too high.

Mum gasps, but stands still like someone's frozen her.

Syd screams with delight and the driver does it again, and again.

He stops, looks at me, and throws Syd miles into the sky, until Syd's squealing like a piglet and I'm nearly ready to rummage in the bag for the scrapbook, in fact I'm just starting to bend round to the zip when I hear Syd's feet running on the concrete drive again.

I can't take much more of this.

I turn back towards the car and grab Syd's dungarees as he stamps past.

"Take the little fella in the car one day, he can sit in his car seat, come on our rounds," says the chauffeur.

"Yes," says Mum doubtfully.

And the driver taps the side of his nose and winks at me again.

I hang on to Mum's shirt until the car slides quietly out of the drive and along the avenue. Mum grips my hand, very tightly, and picks up Syd by the straps of his dungarees.

"Come on, you two, let's watch a film with Ellie till Uncle Derek gets back."

You're a Good Man, Derek Green

Uncle Derek takes us to school in the morning. In the police car. The lady mayoress's car is parked in the lay-by opposite. "After school, don't go on the bus. Wait in the playground if I'm late, but I won't be," he tells us.

He parks in front of the lady mayoress's car, gets out and stares at it doubtfully as we go into the school gates, then he goes to Mrs Mason's office. "To have a word."

From our classroom, I see his car speed down the road, and we sit, flicking paper pellets, waiting for a teacher.

In the end, it's Mrs Mason who comes in, and for once we actually learn something – I mean, did you know that you can grow crystals from salty water? Or that the first animal in space was a dog?

Mrs Gayton seems to have left the school. She's not even been mentioned. Sam Lewis sticks up his hand in the middle of an argument about Louis Armstrong the musician and Neil Armstrong the spaceman. "Miss? Miss? What's happened to Mrs Gayton? Is it true that she's really a man?"

Mrs Mason pinches her lips and shows us a picture of moon craters.

Just before break, Mrs Mason says: "Ellie, Scarlett, my office please, now."

Ellie stares at me and I shrug – I don't think we've actually done anything wrong recently, although I suddenly start to worry about Uncle Derek, who was definitely acting strangely this morning – has he found out about the sweet-shop raid? Has he told Mrs Mason?

I think about Uncle Derek stuck on his own on a tiny island in the middle of the sea.

With no watch or phone or stopwatch.

Mrs Mason, too.

We follow Mrs Mason out across the playground.

221

I grab an apple from the fruit basket in the corridor. I don't really mean to eat it; I just feel the need to hold something.

I glance towards the road. The lady mayoress's car is still sitting there. I take a bite of the apple, feebly hoping to hide behind it.

Mrs Mason pushes open the door to her office.

I nearly choke.

There, on a chair, sits Mrs Gayton. She's wearing a proper tracksuit, one that covers up her legs, and she's gripping a box of chocolates.

"Right, girls, Mrs Gayton has something to say to you," says Mrs Mason, edging behind her desk. She puts her hand out as an invitation to Mrs Gayton.

Mrs Gayton screws up her face. Her teeth show, and she pulls back her painted red lips in a way that suggests someone dying in extreme pain.

It's a smile.

"Girls," she says. "Tha … Thanks." She holds the box of chocolates out in front of her; it quivers at the end of her bony arm. "I'm … very … grateful."

Ellie sashays forward and takes the chocolates, taking care not to touch Mrs Gayton's scary fingers.

"Thank you, Mrs Gayton, I'm glad we were able to help."

I just stand with my mouth open.

What?

Mrs Gayton said "thanks"?

To us????!!!??

What?

"And?" says Mrs Mason.

"Scarlett," says Mrs Gayton. "I must apologise for my attitude to you." She looks up at Mrs Mason.

I can see the words really hurt her.

Mrs Mason's talking again. "So, girls, now, if you want to see Mrs Gayton, she'll be working on the pier – isn't that wonderful?"

"Yes," I say, wondering what she's talking about.

"Well," says Ellie. "That's very exciting, Mrs Gayton. All-in wrestler – who'd have thought it?"

We're sleeping back at our house for the first time since the burglary. Mum's tidied up my bedroom and burned a scented candle so it smells of fake lemons instead of scene-of-crime officers. They broke my bedside moon lamp, so Mum's bought me a jazzy blue one that seems more grown up, but it feels strange.

Ellie's doing her homework, it was set about five minutes ago, but she likes to clear it out of the way, "so that I can enjoy the rest of the weekend". I'll do mine at bedtime on Sunday night. Ellie will get ten out of ten. I would normally get "Could try harder" in Mrs Gayton's scrawl, but perhaps this time I *will* try harder, to please Mrs Mason.

That would be the *right* thing to do.

I'm staring at the ceiling trying to think of good things, and I'm trying not to let the pair in the lady mayoress's car worry me. Just at the moment, we're all in the house, Uncle Derek too, so we're safe.

Good things.

The best good things are the ones that you've done for other people. I mean, Mrs Gayton has been living a lie, but when we rescued her, we did the right thing, even though she's been doing the wrong thing for years. She was lucky we were there, she was lucky Ellie's dad sent us on a lifesaving course, and she was lucky the lifeguard knew how to get the whistles off from round her neck, or she'd have been strangled.

She was lucky there was a job for an all-in wrestler at the end of the pier. I don't even know what an all-in wrestler is – it just sounds like the right thing for Mrs Gayton.

She's also lucky I could forgive her.

"Ellie?"

"Yes — are you thinking about Mrs Gayton?"

"I am," I say. "But we did the right thing."

"Oh yeah," she says. "Scarlett?"

"Yes?"

"Would you rather it was Mrs Gayton, or Melissa and Jessica at the bottom of the pool?"

I think about it for a minute. "All of them?"

Ellie laughs. "Me too."

I listen to the rumbling of Mum and Uncle Derek talking downstairs.

I'm still trying to think about Mrs Gayton, but my mind keeps wandering back to the lady mayoress.

Ellie's doing a long page of maths. I take out my book bag and flick through to the homework.

It swims in front of my eyes.

I can't do it.

Mum and Uncle Derek are chatting in the kitchen. They think they're being quiet. I slip out of the bedroom and sit at the top of the stairs, listening.

It's mostly boring, about Syd's nursery and

Mum's job, but then he says: "I'm sorry I don't measure up to Richard very well, you must think me a poor second best."

"You're a good man, Derek Green," Mum answers.

"But Richard earned all that money, and gave it away. What a thing to do!" Then Uncle Derek must turn around, because he becomes harder to hear. "You don't think he drove himself off that cliff on purpose – to protect other people?"

"I've thought of that, but who?"

"You and Scarlett?"

There's a long silence. Houdini climbs the stairs to doze on my lap. I slip down one more tread so that I can hear better.

"Who was he protecting us against?" asks Mum.

Uncle Derek takes a long time to reply. "Queenie, and her gang, the ones that didn't get caught."

"Queenie?" Mum sounds sad. "I was afraid you'd say that. I wanted to think she was just a figment of someone's imagination, but she's not, is she? Could I have seen her, Derek? Recently?"

Someone starts to chop something on a board. The knife echoes up the stairs.

"Yes, I think you probably could have. Sadly she's

not a figment of anyone's imagination," says Uncle Derek. "And she didn't go to South America either, all two hundred pounds of her is alive and well and watching TV with our faces plastered all over it."

"How do you know it's her? I thought no one had ever seen her?" asks Mum.

"The last couple of days I've been poking around, asking questions, talking to the Metropolitan Police, and I'm pretty sure it's her."

"Isn't there anyone who'd testify against her?"

Uncle Derek laughs. "Testify against her? No way – the person who told me what she looked like asked to join the witness protection scheme. There's no way I can get anyone to stand up in court against them. I've got to catch them red-handed."

"So, she was our burglar?" asks Mum.

"Her brother," says Uncle Derek. "Her brother, the chauffeur."

You're Nearly There

Uncle Derek's told us to stay indoors. Which is a shame because today is the hottest day of the summer so far. On the other hand, I have no desire to run into Queenie and her brother, if that's who they are.

I haven't told Ellie about the conversation I overheard. I don't want to scare her. It's bad enough being scared on my own, I need her to be normal.

"Why, Dad?" asks Ellie.

He fingers his moustache. "Some undesirables around, girls, better if you stay in the house for now." He fiddles with my window blind, stopping the sun from baking the bedroom, although it's already boiling and stinks of warm washing powder.

Ellie lies on the floor and stares at the ceiling. I tuck my legs over the end of the top bunk and hang upside down so that my hair just touches the floor.

"Where's Mum?" I ask.

"Downstairs, with Syd," he says. "I'll be out in the garden."

"Hmm," says Ellie, reaching for a pile of magazines. She starts flicking through them, so I look around for something to do, anything really, I'd even consider French knitting if I had any wool. I unhook myself from the bunk and slide to the floor. Dad's scrapbook's poking out from under the bed, and the Airfix kit.

I push the Airfix kit towards Ellie, with my foot. She grunts and empties the pieces into an opened magazine. "It's just an aeroplane – why would your dad give you an aeroplane to make?"

"Dunno," I say.

"Got any glue?" she asks.

I point at my top drawer and she goes over to rustle through the pants and socks and badges and rubbish that ends up in there. "Yes," she says, pulling out an encrusted yellow tube.

I open the scrapbook and trawl through it for the millionth time. I practically know it by heart. The first half's full of tales of missing objects returned, the second, stories of gifts to charities. In between, Dad's pasted a load of random things, like the pasty wrapper and the ticket.

"There, that's the cockpit done." Ellie's sticking the model together. "But there seem to be far too many pieces for just one little aeroplane."

I stare at the scrapbook. "Why, Dad, why?"

"What?" says Ellie.

"Nothing, I didn't realise I spoke." But there's something odd about the page I'm looking at. Dad's numbered the pages. This is page nineteen, and he's drawn some little eyes inside the nine, looking down towards the bottom of the page. I turn the page over, it should be page twenty, but it isn't; it's page twenty-two.

Pages twenty and twenty-one are missing.

Ellie's singing Take That songs under her breath and rattling the Airfix plastic.

I look at the edge of the page. I can see now that two sheets of paper are stuck together. My fingernails are too long, Mrs Gayton was always telling me off about them, but this time, they're exactly what I need. I run my thumbnail down the tiny gap in the paper and it makes a quiet cracking sound. Glue giving way? I slip my forefinger nails into the gap and pull.

Crack.

The pages lie apart, and there, in the middle, is a picture of Dad with me as a baby on his shoulders. It's a big picture, and it isn't stuck down.

I stare at it.

I've never seen this photo before. But it was taken here, there's the corner of the house, and in the background the control tower of the aerodrome. The hedges are thick and green and the sky blue. It must have been a day in summer.

I hold the picture and stare into Dad's eyes, those funny, sparky eyes so full of life and laughing.

It's only then that I turn it over.

29 November
Dearest Scarlett,
I'm writing this in the café at Fazackerley Hall, before getting a train back to London. I've been by the house, but I didn't call on you, your mum was busy and you were playing outside the

back door. I don't think you noticed me, but if you did, I'm sorry I couldn't stop and say goodbye. You looked very pretty in your yellow sweater, and I don't expect Mum minded what you'd done to the teapot too much.

By the time you find this, by the time you're old enough to find this — you may even have forgotten about me. If you have, then that's fair enough, I haven't been around as much as a dad should be, but if you haven't, then I hope the things I've left you have helped to fill in some of the gaps, so that you know more about me than you did before.

Choose your friends carefully, don't get into strangers' cars.

Look after yourself, look after your mum, and Scarlett, you're nearly there, you can do it. Just keep looking up.

All my love,
Dad

My Friend
Ellie

I read it six times. I put it down and pick it up and read it again.

"Scarlett?" Ellie says, landing a wonky aeroplane on the floor by my foot. "Are you OK? You've gone completely white."

I hand the photograph to her and stare at the aeroplane she's made. My fingers pick it up and trace the lumps of wet glue on the sides.

He was here, he saw me, the day I filled the teapot with sand and leaves. How long ago was that?

It must have been almost the week before he died. I was five? Maybe six?

Why didn't he call on us?

And then I remember; I filled Mum's teapot with sand and leaves because a plumber was working under the sink. I wanted to play washing-up, but he'd turned the water off and Mum told me to go outside and get water from the water butt, but it was cold and smelled of dead frogs. For a second, completely unreasonably, I hate the plumber because he stopped me seeing my dad for the last time.

Mum got really cross about her teapot. The tea was gritty all through Christmas.

"Scarlett," Ellie says, staring at the letter in my hands. "Whoa." Her eyebrows have practically disappeared into her hair.

"Yes, it means he was watching us, coming to the house, really soon before he died, but I didn't see him." I'm surprised by tears and try to blink them back under control, but they won't be controlled, they just keep coming. I turn to wipe my nose on the duvet cover, but it isn't enough.

"Oh, Scarlett." Ellie puts her arm over my shoulder; it's funny, I can tell she's not really putting her weight behind it, but it's nice all the same. "It must be awful not having a dad."

I sniff. "It must be hard not having a mum. I can't imagine it."

We sit leaning against each other while the rush of tears slows, Ellie holding up the photo, and me still wiping my face on the duvet cover. She flips it over, and we both read the message one more time.

"*You're nearly there ... Just keep looking up...*" says Ellie. "What does he mean?"

Nearly there.

Nearly there?

"Does he mean we've nearly found something?" I say, really really quietly.

Ellie shrugs, then grins. "Some leftover diamonds? Maybe?"

"Scarlett! Ellie!" It's Mum, calling up the stairs, her feet just starting to thump on the treads. "Do you fancy some orange juice or something?"

We jump to our feet. I stuff the picture back in the scrapbook and slide it under the bed as if we were doing something wrong.

Mum sticks her head round the door. I look at the floor, playing with the pieces of the Airfix kit. I don't want Mum to see that I've been crying.

"Phew – a bit hot in here, isn't it?" says Mum, flapping her arms at the fug of Ellie and the fabric conditioner.

"Can we go outside?"

Mum's face wrinkles as she comes to a decision.

"Oh, go on then."

Another Letter

We take the Airfix kit down with us, and sit at a little table in the shade, fiddling with the pieces. We've still only got an aeroplane and a pile of random rods.

Uncle Derek's trying to mow the grass with Mum's electric lawnmower, but it doesn't really mow so much as chew. I think all the tyre tracks are probably making it more difficult.

Mum's putting new bean sticks in her vegetable patch.

Ellie's struggling with the pile of spare Airfix pieces. There are eight girders, some random discs, eight sides that almost make an octagonal shed, and a roof of sorts. Perhaps they really were just leftovers in the kit or maybe Ellie made the aeroplane so badly that she missed out all these essential parts.

But what aeroplane has a shed on it?

There has to be a reason.

I fly the little aeroplane over the table and land it on a leaf.

What on earth did Dad give me this for? Did he want me to become a pilot? Did he want to *be* a pilot? Was he not really a spy at all but in the Airforce, dropping bombs on someone? That wouldn't have been good at all.

"Oh, Scarlett, I've just remembered," says Mum. "There's a letter for you, on the hall table; it must have been delivered this morning." She pushes back a hair from her forehead. "Sorry, I should have told you earlier."

A letter – for me? I never get letters.

I pop back inside the house, which seems completely pitch-black after the brightness of outside, and stumble into the hall. There's a white envelope, but no stamp.

Hand-delivered and it's been written on a

computer.

I turn it over and hold it up against the light coming through the glass front door.

Hmm.

Probably something to do with school?

I tear open the flap and there's a tiny flash as I do so. Have you ever noticed that about envelopes, they flash? Anyway this one does and I pull open the letter.

Dear Scarlett
We think it's time we got this sorted.
Shall we say 8p.m.?
After that ... well...
Things might happen.
Love
Us
x

Look

I take the letter out to Ellie.

She reads it and I feel sick.

"We should show Dad," she says. "It's a threat."

"We should."

"But you'll have to tell him about the sweets — and your mum — because we have to come clean about all of it, and the scrapbook and Fazackerley, and all the things that were in the box. All of it."

I think about Mum's reaction to the penguins and I imagine her reaction to the sweets. She won't like that I've kept secrets from her and there are so many.

"I'm not sure I've got the courage."

Ellie looks up at me. She points at Syd, who's playing in mud again. "Really? With him at stake?"

"They're not going to come now, not with your dad standing here," I say. "It's just that Dad left all this for me to solve. Whatever's at the end of the trail, it's mine, and I've got to find it. Later, if we haven't worked it out, I promise I'll tell them at supper."

Ellie glares at me over her glasses. "I'll hold you to it. If you don't, I will."

I swallow.

Mum suggests we go for a swim, and like a condemned man, I imagine this as my last treat on this earth. The water looks especially clear, especially inviting. The sun sparkles so beautifully on the surface. It makes me feel sad.

Sad because I might not get to the end of the chase. I feel as though Queenie and her brother have already beaten me. Not that they'll find whatever it is Dad's left, I'm not going to give them what they want, but I'm sorry that Uncle Derek's going to have to deal with them, I'm sad because I still don't understand what Dad wanted me to do.

I'm pretty sure he didn't want me to steal sweets, or rescue penguins.

He might have been pleased that I dragged crabby old teachers from the bottom of the pool, but that was more to do with chance and Uncle Derek than Dad.

He couldn't have expected me to give huge sums of money to charity, because I'm only eleven and I've only got my pocket money.

Just keep looking up.

I stare up into a cloudless blue sky.

We take ten minutes blowing up lilos, partly because Syd keeps sitting on them and all the air comes out instead of going in. They're all sweaty and sticky, and mine's got sand and algae on it from last summer and smells of wellington boots.

Ellie's excited, so I try really hard to be happy too, stuffing the thought of the row to come out of my head.

We run to the tank and float the lilos on the water.

"This is the scary bit," I say and clamber on to my lilo.

I last about a second before Ellie tries to get on to hers and tips us both in. I go right under and

I am probably dead, the water's so cold. My feet press against the disturbing slimy things on the bottom and I push myself up, popping up to the surface.

Ellie's still trying to climb on to her lilo. "Ha, ho, ha!" she yelps.

It's so cold the water forces all the air out of my lungs and I have to clamber out and cough on the side.

Ellie swims to the side; her lips have already gone blue. I give her a hand out of the water.

"Oh," she says, juddering. "That's the coldest water I've ever been in."

"Great, isn't it?"

"Fab," she says, and tries again. Her skin's lobster veined with white, from the cold, and my bathing costume's really too small for her. She balances on her hands and knees on the lilo, the water creeping in across the top. "S'freezing," she yelps. Then she throws her weight forward and shoots across the tank.

She bobs gently, and shuffles herself forward until she's lying flat, resting her chin on the back of her hands.

"Brilliant," she says.

My teeth chattering, I jump, throwing one leg on either side of my lilo. It's a risky strategy, but although I get utterly soaked, and nearly tip up, I just cling on and wriggle until I'm lying on my back, looking up.

The sky's still utterly blue. Not a single cloud. Just a seagull hovering miles above me. I close my eyes and float.

Ellie's singing. It's the theme from *Stardust.* I think.

When I open my eyes again, I try to work out where I am, which way round. I push my foot against the side, and shoot backwards across the tank.

The sky whizzes over me. I can see the chimney of our house on one side, and the control tower of the airfield on the other.

And then I sit up, feeling hot and cold all at once.

"Ellie?"

She goes on singing.

"Ellie."

"What?"

I point at the control tower.

"What about it?"

"What does it look like to you?"

"A control tower?"

"A shed, on legs. The Airfix kit, the leftovers?"

Ellie stares.

"Oh," she says. "Oh!"

Up

We don't bother to get dressed. Anyway, that would raise suspicion. We abandon the lilos on the tank, and in our swimsuits, tiptoe through the gap in the hedge behind the watercress beds and stumble into the airfield.

The control tower looks exactly like a shed balanced on a pyramid of girders.

"What are we looking for?" says Ellie, panting over the grass.

"I don't know, we're just looking up."

It doesn't take long, it isn't far away. There's a huge red sign saying KEEP OUT and some barbed-wire balls, but someone's cut a path through and we pick our way past without tearing ourselves to pieces. In retrospect, clothing might have been a good idea, but it's too late now. We stop under the legs of the tower and stare up.

I've hoped that "up" would be obvious. But when I look up, all I can see is the underside of the tower. There's a rusty ladder from the ground to a small trapdoor.

"Scarlett?" says Ellie doubtfully.

I put my foot on the first rung of the ladder. It's hot from the sun, but feels solid, so I climb the next and so on.

"Scar-lett," calls Ellie.

But I keep going until I can reach the trapdoor, which is held closed by a padlock. A small rusty padlock, but a padlock all the same.

Rats.

So this is why he gave me his tools. Not for penguins, or sweets, but for the airfield.

Rats, rats, rats.

"What is it?" calls Ellie.

"A padlock."

"Oh, pooh," she says. "Shall I go back for your dad's tools?"

"No — you'll get caught. We'll have to think of something else. Can you find a rock?"

Ellie starts searching around on the ground; there's nothing but grass and tarmac. But at the edge of the airfield there's a pile of old farm equipment rusting by the hedge.

"There!" I point. "A bar, or anything?"

I start to clamber back down the ladder. The metal rungs are hard on my feet, so Ellie reaches the pile of rubbish long before I make the bottom of the ladder.

"Here!" she shouts. She's waving a thing like a crowbar. "Will this do?"

I clamber up the ladder again, this time much more conscious of only wearing a swimsuit. The ladder's rusty and my knees scrape against the rough metal, and I've nowhere to carry the iron bar. I have to jam it under my armpit until I reach the top. I wobble it above my head until it wedges through the loop that the padlock's attached to. I twist it round and the wood splinters, letting the screws of the loop loose.

"Mind out!" I shout and throw the bar to the ground.

There's a piece of wood acting as a fastener, so

I twirl it round and the trapdoor above my head becomes heavy. I have to duck to let it open.

I look down at Ellie. "I'm going in. Do you want to come?"

"No thanks, I'll be a lookout."

She makes a thumbs up and, with a mixture of fear and excitement, I hoist myself up through the opening.

Dad

It's exactly like a shed. An octagonal shed with an amazing view, all the way over to the sea, and back to our garden. It's even more like a shed because it's filled with old rubbish. Although all the walls have windows, someone's hung things on nails above them, so the view's spotted with gas masks and ancient furry jackets and it's all smothered in cobwebs.

In the middle of the space, next to the trapdoor, is a huge desk piled high with old electrical stuff, dials and knobs and wires as if someone started to empty the place but gave up when they realised they'd have to lug it all down the ladder.

Under one of the windows, the one that faces towards our house, lies a much more modern rucksack, and a toolkit. I pick up the rucksack and shake the contents on to the floor.

"What have you found?" shouts Ellie, from below.

"Nothing much," I say.

There's glue, paper, scissors, a brand-new sweatshirt, still with tags on, an empty water bottle, a torch, a teach-yourself Mandarin Chinese book, an empty sandwich box and a pair of binoculars. Wedged in the bottom, there's one of those sleeping bags that squeeze into impossibly tiny bags, and a high-tech inflatable mattress in the shape of a coffin.

He slept up here?

I pick up the binoculars. Dad's? I look through them. The wood on the side of the shed looks very big, the floorboards so close that they're out of focus. I lift the binoculars so that I'm looking through the window and point them towards our garden. Fantastic – I can see mice running along the edge of the compost heap. I can see Uncle Derek changing into his tracksuit in Mum's bedroom, my bedroom curtains, closed against the sun, and Mum cutting bread in the kitchen. I can even see what Syd's watching on TV.

I stare through the binoculars at my brother moving around in the house.

So he watched us. He saw me, all the time. He'd have seen me getting up in the morning, going to bed at night. He'd have watched me go to school on the first day, in Mum's car, wearing my first school uniform. He must have seen the plumber under the sink, Mum fussing about, trying to make tea. He'd have watched it from here, the day he wrote the letter. I look around, and there's a biro lying on the dusty desk, with a few sheets of yellowed paper.

I blow the dust away. There in Dad's writing are a mass of false starts. The letter, written a hundred times in different ways: *Scarlett love, Darling Scarlett, My dearest little one…*

All written while I played outside in the garden with Mum's teapot and the leaves. I collect up all the paper.

"Scarlett — are you all right?" yells Ellie from below.

"Sorry — yes, but I haven't found it yet. Whatever it is."

"Look up?" she says.

I do look up.

There's another trapdoor. Not locked, but there's no way of getting up there, no ladder.

I pull the chair across the wooden floor until it's underneath the trapdoor and stand on tiptoes. I can just reach the bolt. It takes several goes to get it to slide across but in the end, the trapdoor slams open, showing a rectangle of blue sky.

The roof slopes, so I place my fingers over the lower edge of the opening and pull myself up. It hurts, the prickly stuff on the outside of the roof digs into my fingers and I nearly let go, but just manage to hang on long enough to throw my shoulders over the edge of the opening. I balance for an age to get my breath back before scraping the rest of my body through the hole.

This is high up. I look down the slope of the roof; there's a small railing around the side, but it's been there for a horribly long time and I don't suppose it would stop me falling. Keeping my fingers on the hatchway, so that if I feel dizzy I can fall back into the room below, I look up and around. Above me, a short ladder leads to a mass of antennae and small things that look like satellite dishes. They're all grey and ancient.

Keep looking up.

"Scarlett!" Ellie's voice, but really far away now. I know she's not warning me about Uncle Derek and Mum, they're still in the house, I can see shapes moving about in the kitchen.

"Yes – I'm on top now."

But I can't hear her answer. Now I'm up here, it's as if the sounds come from further away – there's a tractor in a field over at Dampington, a load of seagulls circling the zoo, children playing in the park, a car engine quite close, probably Uncle Derek going to work, and the really close sound of the antennae rubbing against each other. The sun's warm on my skin, but there is a breeze up here.

What an excellent place.

Perhaps that's what Dad wanted me to find; a new point of view.

Keep looking up.

There's nothing above but the old metalwork, and probably an even better view.

I turn really slowly, my feet still kicking in the empty room below and bend my back until I can sit on the edge of the trapdoor. From here I can crawl up the prickly roofing cover to the ladder.

I try not to think about down. But I can't help imagining Ellie underneath the tower, tiny, and me on top, also tiny, and the distance between me and the ground: vast. And the ground underneath isn't exactly bouncy, and there isn't a safety net.

So instead I think about Dad.

Dad sitting up here with his binoculars.

Dad crawling over the roof, the little sharp green edges of the roofing digging into his knees.

Dad sleeping in the tower, eating sandwiches, learning Chinese; living as close to us as he could, waiting for his next mission.

I wonder if Mum knew he was there? I imagine her signalling to him out of the window, meeting him by the big tank in the dark.

And then I look out across the fields and try to get inside Dad's head.

I don't think she knew he was there. I think it was a secret, to keep us safe. I think he did everything to keep us safe.

The ladder feels strong. When I pull on it, it doesn't flex. Safe? I think about some of the gym equipment at school. It's probably about the same age.

Putting my left foot on the bottom rung I haul

the rest of my body up until I'm standing on it and can lock my arms around the top.

From here, I can see the sea.

There's a ferry coming into the harbour, followed by a huge crowd of seagulls.

This is an even better view; I can practically see the Isle of Wight.

Keep looking up.

So I look up.

One tall grey mast.

One short grey mast. Covered in lichen.

Two meshy square things on sticks.

One large grey satellite dish, catching the light.

One large grey satellite dish, not catching the light.

I look again.

The satellite dish that's catching the light is really bright.

Ridiculously bright.

I'm not going to get excited, but I'll take a look, just to be sure.

I climb the ladder so that my arms are above it; there isn't really anything to hang on to now, except the antennae. I hold the taller antennae, and rub my fingers across the middle of the satellite dish.

It's lumpy.

Really gently, I pick at one of the lumps, it comes away in my hand and I stare at it.

My Girls

I pluck eight diamonds from the dish, stuff them inside my swimsuit and pick my way down the ladder. My heart's pumping crazily, I'm not sure if it's the height or the diamonds, and I have to stop several times on my way down the roof.

When I reach the trapdoor, I drop through on to the floor and look around for something to hold the diamonds. Dad's backpack, just the thing.

I slip the diamonds into the smallest pocket and stop.

I could take the backpack up with me, and some pliers from the toolkit to help pick off the rest of the diamonds.

Or I could rush down and show Ellie, and Mum and Uncle Derek, and I could tell Mum about the sweets and give her these diamonds at the same time.

I can wait for the rest of the diamonds.

Dad's backpack's big, so it's hard to get through the trapdoor, and I have to take the rungs really slowly because it feels like I'm being pulled backwards.

"Ellie, I've found them, they're up on the satellite dish, there must be loads. I've got some here."

There's no answer, I look around, but I can't see her.

"Ellie?"

I keep climbing down, slowly, one rung at a time, although I'd love to put my feet on either side and whizz down like a fireman.

I'm nearly at the bottom. "Ellie?"

"Scarlett." A hand touches me on the shoulder.

I stop.

That isn't Ellie, and it isn't Uncle Derek either.

I look round.

The chauffeur. He's holding the backpack, even though I'm still wearing it.

"Thanks, Scarlett," he says. "Saved us a lot of bother."

"Where's Ellie?" I say.

"Safe, if you cooperate. How many did you get?"

I shrug. "I don't know what you're talking about."

"Don't be silly, girly. What you got in that backpack? Eh?"

He closes one hand round my wrist and I pull away, but he's much stronger than me.

Something moves behind him, it's the big black car and the lady mayoress is at the wheel, but she can't drive through the barbed wire.

"Where's Ellie?" I cry, leaning back, but going nowhere, my feet can't grip enough to get away.

" 'Urry up, you idiot – get the brat in," the huge woman shouts from the car.

She throws the back door open and I see Ellie inside, tied up in sweaters.

"Help!" I yell, still clinging to the backpack. I know my voice'll be lost in the seagulls. But I try again. "HELP!"

"Heeeeelllllpppppp!" screams Ellie at the top of her voice. "Daaaaaad!!!"

"Shut up!" says the man, trying to get me through the gap in the wire. I kick, but with no shoes he doesn't seem to notice and I'm losing ground, although I've still got the backpack.

He lifts me off the ground and carries me through the wire until we're almost at the car.

"Dadddddd!" yells Ellie, impressively loudly, and the woman stuffs a stocking in her mouth.

"HELP!" I shout, and pull the pocket on the side of the bag with my teeth. Using my knee, I flip the bag over to tip the diamonds on to the ground. Even there, on the tarmac they glow. The man stops – caught between rescuing the diamonds and bundling me into the car.

It's as if the world's stopped, they're both staring, and Ellie too, and although I'd love nothing better than to watch the evening sun dancing on the diamonds, I take my chance and sink my teeth as hard as I can into his arm.

"Yow!" he screams.

Ellie rolls from the car, spluttering, but despite her size the woman leaps to grab her, whisking her up in the air and dumping her back in the car.

I bite harder; his flesh feels weird under my teeth.

"DEVIL CHILD!" the man bellows, kicking at me. He lands one on my foot. I nearly let go, but clamp my jaws down on his arm, feeling his skin rupture.

"GET OFF!" he yells, running backwards towards the barbed wire. "OW!" The wire snags the back of his head.

I let go and run in the direction of home. We need help.

A figure in black springs towards me, over our garden hedge. "HEY!" It's Uncle Derek. "YOU – LEAVE MY GIRLS ALONE!" He moves so fast that the chauffeur seems to be in slow motion, his legs striding out, but getting nowhere, before Uncle Derek throws him to the ground.

I turn and sprint in the direction of the car. I don't know what I can do about stopping it, but the lady mayoress is scrabbling on the tarmac, trying to pick up the diamonds, she hasn't made it back into the driving seat yet.

"Hey!" I yell.

She turns, breaking her stride, and I skip past and jump into the driving seat. I slam the door and push down the lock. For a moment she just stares before grabbing the door handle, her eyes burning with fury through the glass. Behind her I can see Uncle Derek trying to get handcuffs on the chauffeur.

I reach down with my feet. Two pedals. One must be go, one must be stop. I put my hands on the wheel and press the right-hand one.

The barbed wire makes a horrible noise along the side of the car.

Such a shame about the paintwork.

But lovely watching the lady mayoress run for her life.

As we follow her slowly round the air field, and chase her back to Uncle Derek, I think about the words in my ear.

My girls, he said.

My girls.

I like the sound of that.

And What Did I Do
with Them?

It's perfectly true that Mum nearly completely exploded when we told her about stealing the sweets and the toys, and following Dad's trail across the countryside, but when she saw all the diamonds lying in the fruit bowl, she lost some of the really hot fury and simply simmered for the evening.

Then she cried and hugged me and told me she loved me, and told me off once more, and I wondered again how Ellie could possibly manage without a mum.

Uncle Derek thought it wasn't a good idea for me to go up and pick the rest of the diamonds from the dish, which was a shame, because we had to wait for some climbing friends of his to come back from holiday and go up with ropes and safety nets and helmets. In the meantime, he camped at the bottom of the tower, and Ellie and I joined him.

It was fun. We fried sausages and eggs in a police frying pan and ate them off police plates.

The climbing friends brought down the diamonds and handed me a small sandwich box that they found taped to the back of the satellite dish.

Uncle Derek paused, a sausage sandwich poking past his moustache as he watched me open it.

There was a dead rose, and another letter.

A badly written one, on a sheet of paper like the ones in the control tower.

Scarlett,

I'm so sorry that you'll have to go through so much to get this, but I want you to have the diamonds, and I want you to decide what happens to them. I'm hoping that you've learned enough about me to help you make that decision wisely. I wanted to give you these myself, in years to come, but just at the moment, it looks as though that's not going to happen.

You probably wonder whether these diamonds are mine to give. They are, they're my wages from the state — I've earned them, no matter what anyone may say.

If it's you, Scarlett, reading this, then you and I have succeeded, I've left you the right messages, and you've been enough like me to understand them. With any luck, it's been a happy journey of discovery that will help you with the next part of your life.

Goodbye, sweetheart.

I love you, but don't let that stop you from loving other people,

Dad

After that, Uncle Derek kept the diamonds at the police station in case anyone stepped forward to claim them. He said that even though Dad had left a sort of a will, ownership was still hazy but that possession was nine tenths of the law. I'd no idea what he meant, but no one did come forward, so he gave them back to me.

There were one hundred and forty-four of them.

Twelve twelves.

A gross.

A gross of diamonds.

I put them in piles in my room. Ellie and I had a

diamond dinner for Barbie and Ken.

We let Syd push them round with a digger.

We glued them to our ears with wallpaper paste; we looked mad.

Then I stuck them all round the window frames in my bedroom with Blu-tack.

They made pretty patterns on my bedroom ceiling and I tried to imagine myself wearing them round my neck as a dazzling twenty-one-year-old, sweeping around a dance floor with some old-fashioned prince.

Then I'd look at my grubby feet and tatty jeans and feel a bit weird.

It took about a week to decide what to do.

The money sent the penguins to a lovely zoo in Canada. It also sent the monkeys to America and the flamingos to Gloucestershire.

It paid Mr Hammond for all the spoiled watercress. It bought Ellie some nice new clothes, without sparkles, Syd a box of cars, Mrs Gayton, a stretchy suit in her new life as an all-in wrestler, and Mum, a luxury holiday for five in the Greek Islands.

The rest?

I kept the three smallest diamonds, to make into that necklace, and I sponsored Uncle Derek to run the London Marathon.

He raised over a million pounds.

It was only about two days after that, that he and Ellie moved in.

Acknowledgements

I'd like to thank the people who helped Scarlett's journey: many friends and family have been very supportive, but I would like to thank in particular my editor, Kirsty Stansfield, for seeing the future for Scarlett, and for caring like a midwife for every sentence; my agents, Pippa and Kate, for their patience; and Amanda for reading and Ian for re-reading drafts of the manuscript and being honest.